THE
NEW
NEIGHBOURS

JOANNE RYAN

Tamarillas Press

Cover Design: © Joanne Ryan
ISBN: 978-1-913807-18-4

Other books by Joanne Ryan:
Without Reason
All The Lost Years
Not Your Average Girl
The Lodger
The Double
One Night
Lie To Me

Writing as Marina Johnson:
Fat Girl Slim
Fat Girl Slim Returns
Fat Girl Slim Three
A Confusion of Murders
So Talk To Me
The Herb Sisters
Say Hello & Wave Goodbye
The Harriet Way

CHAPTER ONE

There was a man who begged in town that summer; he had long, straggly hair tied back in a ponytail and clothes that were shiny with dirt. A skinny, mournful-looking brown dog would lie next to him on a filthy, once white duvet that we guessed they both used to sleep under at night.

Sometimes, he'd be sitting in the doorway of Frenchams, a large old-fashioned department store that sold everything you could ever want or need. It's long gone now; replaced by new shops that sell cheap birthday cards and bargain toiletries. The security guards from the store never allowed him to stay in the shop doorway for very long before they moved him on.

He put people off.

Shoppers didn't like walking past him because he made them feel uncomfortable with his hungry eyes and dirty clothes. Who wants to be made to feel guilty for carrying bulging carrier bags full of stuff that you've just bought but don't really need? Nobody, that's who.

Mostly, though, he'd settle himself in the underpass that dissected the town centre from the old bus station. As long as he didn't pester anyone, and no one reported him, the police turned a blind eye and left him in peace. People still had to walk past, but they didn't feel so bad because they didn't have to get too close to him. They could walk on the other side of the underpass and ignore him if they wanted.

He'd take off his black woolly hat and lay it out on the ground in front of his duvet and wait for people to throw money in. We never put any money in because we didn't have any, but other people did. It was mostly coppers in there but there was always the shine of a bit of silver, too; probably ten pence pieces. Maybe there were some pound coins, and he took them out. I don't know, I never saw any in there, but who knows? Sometimes people would buy him a McDonald's or a coffee and take it over and put it on the ground next to him, as if they were feeding a dog. I thought that was insulting, giving him food. Give him money so he can spend it himself, I used to think, or give nothing at all. Charity with strings attached. The ones giving him food liked other people to notice; *look at me,* their smug faces said, as they placed it next to him, *I'm being charitable, aren't I great, aren't I kind, what a good person I am, I've bought this poor unfortunate a meal.*

'If you were really desperate,' we'd say to each other as we passed him, 'and you had absolutely nothing, would you sit on the street and beg or would you steal?' We were eleven-years-old and liked to talk about things like that, and it wasn't really a question that needed answering because we were already thieves. Although we never considered the makeup and sweets that we used to shoplift as proper stealing, because where we came from, everyone did it. As far as we were concerned, it wasn't hurting anyone. The shops could afford it and we were poor, so thought we were entitled to it.

We looked at the man with something approaching pity and agreed that we'd never beg and we couldn't understand why he did; why didn't he just help himself from the shops like us? Stealing food was easy. We did it all the time. We couldn't understand why he didn't do it; he'd have to live on cold food, like sandwiches and pasties, but it had to be better than begging.

We'd never beg; never; because neither of us had it in us to ask for anything. Experience had taught us that the answer would always be *no*, or worse. Much worse.

I remember that day and the things we talked about, even now, and it's stayed with me. It was the same old stuff that we always chatted about but, on that day, we kept up a constant stream of pointless conversation. Because if we kept talking, it might stop us from thinking.

About what we were going to do.

Mostly, I try never to think of the past, and mostly, I succeed. But that was just *before*, and now, I almost laugh at my naivety because we had no idea what was in store for us, despite what we were planning to do. We had no clue that our lives were about to change forever, and that it would be the last time that we would ever make that trip into town together.

And that after that day, the next time we'd meet would be over twenty years later.

CHAPTER TWO

I can't tear myself away from the window, even though I tell myself that someone moving into the house across the street is not that interesting. But still I sit and watch, unable to move, my attention fixated on someone else's possessions.

A large, cream sofa emerges from the van and the removal men jolt it onto their shoulders as if it weighs nothing and then march up the driveway to the open front door. They struggle when they reach the entrance, turning the sofa this way and that, before manoeuvring it through the doorway. They disappear from view and I imagine them positioning it in the lounge.

The house is larger than ours; it has an additional bedroom and an extra bathroom and was also for sale when we bought this house six months ago. We viewed it even though we knew we wouldn't be buying it; Brett's salary wouldn't quite stretch to buying it *and* having the lifestyle that we're used to. Yet. Brett's confident that within the next five years he'll be *moving up* at work and then we'll be leaving this street behind for a much larger house with its own grounds.

Brett has a life plan, and so far, it's all worked out as he's predicted. We sold our London flat for a very healthy profit, even more than we expected. It's almost impossible *not* to make a profit in London. It was always the plan to move out of London because Brett doesn't want to bring up a family in the city. He wanted a good-sized house with lots of room and a garden for the children to play in. But not *too* far away; Brett can be at his desk in central London in less than an hour and the train station is within walking distance of our house, meaning that he doesn't have to drive. And it wasn't only Brett who wanted to move out of London. I did too, although my reasons for wanting to do so differed from his.

The house across the street may be larger than ours, but our house is hardly small. We have five bedrooms and a huge ground floor, not to mention a massive garden at the back. The house was perfect when we moved in, as the previous owners had just spent eighteen months and over two-hundred-thousand pounds remodelling it. We didn't have to pick up so much as a paintbrush. Not that Brett would. He admits that he's not hands on and would rather get someone in and pay them to do it properly. But there was no need, because everything had already been done. The three bathrooms and the downstairs toilet were fitted with new top of the range fittings, as was the kitchen. We have huge, bespoke, folding doors that cover one entire wall of the kitchen and we can open them up when the weather is nice and look out over the garden.

I was suspicious that there must be something wrong with the house when we viewed it, because why would they have so much done to it and then move out? It seemed ridiculous to me. *Subsidence,* I whispered to Brett, as we stood in the kitchen admiring the expensive marble work tops. The estate agent couldn't possibly have heard me, but somehow, he knew what I was thinking. Marriage break-up, he announced, was the reason for the sale. The couple had barely completed the work on the house before they divorced and moved out. He was a solicitor, and she was in finance, according to the garrulous estate agent, and weren't we lucky that we didn't have to do a thing to the place? I felt uncomfortable when he told us about their divorce and wondered if there might be some kind of jinx on the house. Brett said not to be ridiculous; they will accept *asking price*, for God's sake, he said, so why *wouldn't* we buy it? I can still remember the estate agent's grin as he informed us that the owners were in a hurry and even though they could get more if they waited, full asking price would secure the sale for us. It made me wonder who the estate agent was working for and when I said this to Brett when we got home, he laughed, and said, *well, himself, of course.*

So, here we are. It *is* a beautiful house and there's plenty of room for the family of four that we'll eventually become, but I can't say that I don't miss the central location of our flat in London. I could walk along the street and around the corner and there were shops, restaurants and coffee shops galore whereas here, aside from a local newsagent, a mini-mart and a cafe, there's very little without getting in the car and driving somewhere. There is a pleasant park at the end of the street, so maybe I should make the effort and start running or at least walking there every day.

I am a bit bored.

The house is perfect and I've spent the last six months making it even more perfect by filling it with new furnishings, but it's done now; there's only so much stuff I can buy. I need to find something else to do to occupy my days, something constructive. It's been nice getting the house how I want it, but I've spun it out for as long as I can. Brett says it's not worth getting a job because soon, I'll have a baby, and then I'll be moaning that I have got no time at all to myself. It's in his life-plan, new house, new baby. A boy first and then a girl. I asked Brett what if we have a girl first? He shook his head and laughed. Not going to happen, he said, my life-plan is never wrong.

I sigh and resume my house-watching. The removal men are back at the lorry and they manhandle an identical sofa to the first from the platform of the van onto the ground and the process of taking it up the driveway and into the house is repeated. What I'd really like to see is who my new neighbours are; they must have arrived before the van because someone opened the door, didn't they? There's a top of the range black BMW parked in the driveway, which I assume belongs to the new owners so they must be in there. I'm wondering if they'll be around my age or older when a woman emerges from the house and walks along in front of the bay window.

She has a mobile phone clamped to her ear and appears to be deep in conversation as she tracks back and forth across the window. I'd hazard a guess that she's around my age. Tall and wafer-thin, her fair hair is scooped up into a ponytail and she's wearing a pair of sweatpants with a t-shirt. She should look scruffy, but somehow, she looks stylish in the way ultra-thin people do; nothing looks bad on them. I move back from the window and stand behind the curtain just in case she should look over. A tall, dark-haired man comes out of the house and walks along to the window. He moves with an effortless grace, despite his size, and he stands and watches the woman. She stops in front of him and looks up at him before ending the call and putting her phone in her pocket. She barely reaches his shoulders. He looks tall like Brett, who's six-foot-two, although, of course, the woman may not be tall at all.

They're a good-looking couple.

Brett and I are a good-looking couple, so maybe we'll become friends with them. Like attracts like, as I've discovered. As this thought crosses my mind, my mobile rings and I jump guiltily, as if I'm doing something wrong. Maybe I am, maybe watching your new neighbours is spying; maybe what I should have done is take a tray of tea and cakes over. Is that the sort of thing people do? I have no idea.

I pick up my phone from the coffee table and tap the button to answer. It's Brett, of course, on his way home. He rings me every day on his way to the station.

'Hi,' I say breezily.

'Hi darling, how's it going?'

'All good. How was your day?'

I hear him sigh. 'Not bad. Barron's been nagging like an old woman, but aside from that, all good. The sooner he retires, the better, the old dinosaur.'

'New neighbours have moved in across the street.'

'Really? Have you met them yet?'

'No, not yet. I glimpsed them and they look young, like us, but no, I haven't spoken to them yet.'

'Yeah?' Brett says, with obvious disinterest. He's not really listening. I know what he's going to ask next before he even utters the words.

'Did you go for your appointment?'

'Yep.'

'And what did he say?' Brett's words are getting

harder to hear now; he's arrived at the station and I hear the blare of the train announcements and the babble of voices. I hear him breathing as he marches along. I imagine him striding purposefully towards the train, the wave of people parting like the red sea to make way for him, although in reality, he'll be fighting his way through.

'He said not to worry.'

'Did he?' He sounds surprised.

'He said six months is nothing. No specialist will even look at me until we've been trying for at least a year.'

There's silence and I know Brett is massively disappointed; he was pinning his hopes on this appointment. He wanted the GP to start tests to find out why I'm not pregnant after six months of trying.

'We could go private. We *should* go private,' he says.

'We could.' I try to keep my voice level and take the emotion out of it. 'But it would be pointless because when I suggested this to Doctor Sanders, he said we'd be wasting our time and money. Six months is nothing and we just have to be patient and it'll happen.'

'Okay,' Brett says, in a *not okay* voice. 'Look, I'm on the platform, so I'd better go. We'll talk when I get home.' He ends the call before I can answer and I throw my mobile onto the sofa. I hope we don't have to talk about it when he gets home. I'm *sick* of talking about it.

Brett expected me to fall pregnant immediately once we started trying; as each month has gone by, his disappointment has increased and he's become more insistent that I visit our GP to start the process of tests. Six months isn't *that* long to try for a baby. I know this because I've Googled it and discovered that 30% of couples trying to conceive do so in the first month, 75% of couples conceive within six months and 90% of couples conceive within a year. 95% of couples conceive within two years. Not that I'll be telling Brett this, I just hope he hasn't Googled it, too.

I think he might have.

I'm sure he will have.

I wonder if he'll notice, as I did, that the percentages don't add up.

I'll tell Brett what Doctor Sanders said, that Google doesn't know the answer to everything. That they're just generalised statistics and don't consider a woman's personal medical history, how long she's been on the pill or how regular her cycle is.

Although I'd be lying, just as I was lying when I said that Doctor Sanders said a specialist wouldn't see me until we'd been trying for a year.

I made that up.

I made the whole appointment up, actually.

The familiar feelings of guilt and disgust for deceiving Brett surge up and after a moment, I push them firmly down. I have a choice; lie to him or have a baby.

There's always a choice in life, even if neither option is appealing.

To stop my mind from returning to my deceit, I wonder why Brett is so convinced that if I'm not getting pregnant, the fault must lie with me. What about him? How does he know he doesn't have a problem that he's not aware of? Perhaps, next time we're talking about it, I'll ask him. Maybe I'll suggest that he get himself tested and see how he likes it.

I raise my arms and stretch them up to the ceiling. They feel stiff from standing in one position at the window, spying on my new neighbours. I'll go into the kitchen and start cooking something delicious and then maybe, just maybe, Brett will forget to nag about us having a baby the very minute he walks through the door.

I go out into the hallway, which is my favourite part of the house, and stop for a moment and look around. It's light and spacious and the evening sun streaming through the coloured glass in the front door throws crazy patterns onto the walls. The floor tiles are a black and white chequerboard pattern and the ornate, old-fashioned staircase is painted a glossy white. Along one wall is a coat closet, which is basically a long, built-in cupboard to hide all the coats and umbrellas and other paraphernalia away. The previous owners have thought of everything and yet again, I think how sad it is that they got the perfect house, but their marriage failed.

I head along the hallway towards the kitchen and then stop, remembering that I have something else to do before I prepare dinner. I turn and go back to the bottom of the stairs and run up them and along the landing to our bedroom. I go straight through the bedroom and into the dressing room between the bedroom and the ensuite. The dressing room is for both of us, but I have the lion's share of the wardrobes, as I have far more clothes than Brett. I walk to the farthest wardrobe and pull it open; it's full of my jackets and coats hanging neatly side by side. I slip my hand into the pocket of a fake fur coat that sits between a raincoat and a ski jacket, and pull out a small oblong packet. I open the packet and pull out the blister pack of pills and turn them over to check that I have the right day. Satisfied that I haven't missed one, I pop the tiny pill for Tuesday into my mouth. I return the packet to the coat pocket, pushing it right down inside to make sure there's no possibility of it falling out. Not that Brett would ever think to look in my wardrobe; he's not like that.

He trusts me.

I feel the familiar pang of guilt. How much longer can I get away with taking the contraceptive pill when we're supposed to be trying for a baby?

I'll have to make a decision.

Soon.

CHAPTER THREE

I see the new neighbour's car pull up onto their drive across the street and decide to give her ten minutes to get inside before I take the parcel over. When the Amazon delivery driver knocked on my door this morning with their parcel, it didn't surprise me that he'd come to my house even though they have a neighbour next door to them. Most of the people in this street aren't at home during the day. They're busy working at the important and well-paid careers that fund these expensive houses.

When we first moved in, I took in parcels for several of the neighbours, but now I tend not to bother. The first time I took a delivery in, I made the effort and took the next-door neighbours' parcel around to their house in the evening when I knew they'd be home. I thought it would be an opportunity to introduce myself and meet them. The woman who answered the door looked at me blankly when I said that I lived next door and had taken a delivery in for her. She didn't introduce herself and treated me with a disinterest that was bordering on rudeness.

Did I expect gratitude? Yes, I suppose I did, but all I got was a feeling that I was lacking something because I was at home all day and not at work. She treated me as if it were my job to take in her parcels because I had nothing better to do. I refused their parcel the next time the DPD driver arrived at my door; show me some gratitude or collect your parcel yourself.

Maybe I'll get the same reaction from the new people across the road. Just because they're young, it doesn't mean they're going to be any friendlier. But I have to find out because for some bizarre reason my new neighbours fascinate me. I want to get a closer look at them. Maybe it's because they're young and they look sort of glamourous and I've built up a picture in my mind of what they're like. The other people living in this street that I've met in passing are serious and look much older than Brett and me. They make me feel awkward and lacking and I can't imagine having anything in common with them.

Maybe that's how we'll end up one day.

Or perhaps my new neighbours are fascinating me because I have very little else to think about as I rattle around this house on my own all day. Thinking about my new neighbours' beats dwelling on how deceitful I'm being to Brett.

Before I leave the house, I check my appearance

in the large mirror in the hallway at the bottom of the stairs. My hair is pulled up into a casual, messy bun and I've smoothed tinted moisturiser over my face to give myself a bit of colour. Without it, I look washed out. I think I need to get out more and get some fresh air, maybe go for a run or something. Tinted lip moisturiser finishes the look—I thought lipstick was a bit much—and I go over to the closet, open it, and pull out my padded jacket. I pick up my keys from the bowl on the console table, pick up the parcel from the floor, and open the front door. As I step outside and close the door behind me, I'm glad I put on a jacket, even though I only have to walk across the road and up the driveway. The wind is blowing in gusts and it's cold; a typical March day.

At least it's not raining.

I have on what I wear during the day when Brett's at work—sweatpants, a t-shirt and a zip-up workout top. I always change into something decent before he arrives home; a dress or casual trousers and a top, because Brett thinks gym wear should be worn to the gym only. Not that he says that to me, but I've heard him comment enough about other women *slobbing around* to know that he wouldn't like it. I debated getting changed before I took the parcel over, but decided not to even though I haven't *been* to the gym. There's nothing wrong with what I'm wearing and it's pretty much what my new neighbour was wearing the other day. I don't want to look as if I'm made a special effort, because that would just look sad.

I tuck the parcel underneath my arm and walk down our driveway—much shorter than our new neighbours, hardly a driveway at all, really, just a space with shingle underfoot that will fit two cars. We have a privet hedge running along the front and our gates are glossy, black wrought iron ones that most of the other houses in the street have. I open one of the gates and then walk across the road. The tree-lined street is empty and as it's a cul-de-sac, there's no traffic passing through. Brett thinks this is the perfect place to bring up a family, but I've never seen a child in this street, not one. Either there are no children living here at all, despite the size of the houses, or they're kept inside their homes or they're in day-care somewhere. It's nothing like when I was a child and we spent every waking moment out of the house, playing in the street or the surrounding areas. Although where I grew up was vastly different to this.

I walk up the new neighbour's driveway. The BMW isn't there today but there's a blue VW Golf parked in front of the garage. I step onto the porch and press my finger on the bell button and wait. I can't hear the bell ringing and I'm wondering if I should press it again, when the door is opened.

My first thought is that she's older than I took her for when I was watching them move in; forty, but a very attractive forty. She's smiling at me; it's a smile that reaches her eyes and it looks genuine.

This is the first time a neighbour has smiled at me properly on this street, and what a sad thing that is. I return her smile and tell her I've taken her parcel in for her and that I live in the house opposite. She claps her hands together excitedly, as if I've told her something wonderful.

'You're our new neighbour? How wonderful! Come in, come in!'

I'm almost in shock that she seems so delighted to meet me. Without waiting for me to respond, she opens the door wider and turns and heads down the hallway, obviously expecting me to follow her. I stand immobile for a second, unused to such a reception, and then step into the house, close the door and fall into step behind her. She keeps up a constant stream of chatter as she leads the way, and I struggle to catch what she's saying. I follow her into a vast kitchen and she walks straight over to the worktop, picks up the kettle and takes it over to the sink and fills it from the tap. I stand in the middle of the kitchen and watch as she replaces it on the kettle base before turning to me.

'How rude of me! I'm Fen! Lovely to meet you!'

She walks towards me and I hold out my hand, but instead of taking it, she pulls me into a hug and kisses me on both cheeks. I try not to stiffen, but I'm unused to such displays of affection from strangers.

'I'm Natalie,' I say, when she releases me. 'I live at number fifteen.'

She stares at me for a moment and then pulls a rueful face.

'I'm sorry, Natalie, you'll have to forgive my over-familiarity. I always forget how formal you English are.'

She speaks with an accent which I can't place, and I wonder if she's Polish.

'It's fine. We can't help being stuffed shirts. It's in our DNA.'

She bursts into laughter and I can't help joining in.

'Come, sit down.' She takes the parcel from me and then loops her arm through mine and steers me towards a tall stool in front of the kitchen island. 'You and I will drink tea and eat cake and get to know each other, yes?'

'Yes,' I say, as I settle myself onto the comfortable seat.

'Wonderful! And I just know that we will be such great friends, you and I.'

❊ ❊ ❊

'I've met our new neighbour.'

'Yeah?'

I hear the bustle of the station in the background as Brett answers me, and I know that any minute he'll be hanging up.

'Yes, she's called Fen. I haven't met her husband yet because he wasn't there. She's really nice, though, very friendly. I took a parcel over to her that came to our house while they were out.'

'You shouldn't take in other people's parcels; we're not the bloody post office.'

I'm about to answer when Brett hangs up; he'll be in the crush to get on the train and have no time for goodbyes. I'm determined not to let his lack of interest about our new neighbours spoil my mood. I've had a nice day today. Fen and I talked for ages and she was so easy to get on with; warm and funny and not in the least bit stuck up. We were so carried away with getting to know each other that I never realised how the time had flown. It was only when I glanced out of the window that I realised the light was fading and when I looked at my watch; it was nearly half-past-five.

'I didn't realise the time!' I jumped off the stool and picked my keys up from the counter. 'I'd better get back.' I didn't say that I had to start dinner because I didn't want to sound like someone who scurried around after her husband because she didn't have a job. I'd already told Fen that I'd taken the opportunity to give up my job when we moved out of London because of all the traveling, missing out the part about trying for a baby. Fen had given me the impression that she did some sort of work for her husband's company, but didn't elaborate nor seem particularly interested in talking about work.

'Time goes so quickly when you have someone good to talk to,' Fen said.

'Thank you for the tea and the cakes. They were

delicious.'

'My pleasure. It's nice that you eat; so many women I know starve themselves to stay thin.' She smiled. 'You are lucky that you are naturally slim.'

I laughed and took the intended compliment without telling her the truth. She wasn't to know that I exist on practically nothing all day and eat my one meal with Brett in the evening. Keeping as slim as I am takes effort and denial, and sometimes, especially today, I wonder if it's worth it and why I'm doing it. Maybe if I started doing some exercise, I could eat normally instead of half-starving myself.

'We are the same,' she said, as she jumped off the stool. 'I can eat and eat and eat and never put on so much as an ounce. I think we are like sisters—only I am so much older than you!'

'Of course you're not,' I said, picking up my coat from the back of the chair.

'How old are you? Twenty-five? I am forty-four. In fact, I am probably old enough to be your mother.'

'I'm thirty-one,' I said with a laugh. 'And there's no way you look forty-four or anywhere near old enough to be my mother.'

Fen's hand flew to her mouth and she looked at me wide-eyed.

'Please forgive me for saying such a stupid thing. I'm so sorry.'

'Don't be sorry.' I slipped my coat on. 'I got over it a long time ago and I have a happy life now with

Brett.'

'But it's so sad.'

'Honestly, forget it. Other people go through much worse.' I zipped up my coat. 'You must come over to me,' I said. 'And I'll make a cake.'

As Fen led the way down the hallway to the front door, for the first time since I'd arrived, it fell silent. Maybe I'd misread the situation; taken politeness for a desire to be friends. The crushing disappointment that I felt was completely out of proportion to the situation. What is wrong with me? But I know; I felt a connection with Fen, that special something that is rare between two women. The connection that tells me there could be genuine friendship between us, not ladies who lunch or gym friends, or good neighbours, but real friends. It hit me that maybe I'd got it all wrong, and she's friendly like this with everyone she meets because some people are naturally welcoming and outgoing.

'I think,' Fen said, as we reached the front door. 'That I would love to come and visit you. But Natalie, please let me apologise again for my stupid slip of the tongue. It is a fault of mine; to speak first and think later. I'm sorry.'

'Honestly, it's fine.' I wished I hadn't told her about my parents, or lack of them, then. I'm not normally so forthcoming. Fen smiled and patted my arm.

'Now, go home and tell your husband that you have met your mad neighbour. Tell him you are both invited for dinner so that we can all become great friends.'

She opened the door and then turned and threw her arms around me and hugged me.

'I'll talk to Darius tonight and we'll arrange something, yes?' she said, as she released her hold of me.

'That sounds like a plan,' I said, as I stepped outside. 'I'll look forward to it.'

'Perfect! And when the talk turns boring, as it does with men, we'll have each other to talk to, won't we?' She laughed and I joined in. As I walked down their long driveway, I was still smiling because I sensed that Fen and I *would* become friends and I hadn't misread the situation at all.

I'll admit that I'm lonely; I have Brett, but other than him, I have only the wives and girlfriends of *his* friends, and that's not healthy. Some of my work colleagues and I were friendly, but since I left, I haven't bothered with any of them, or them with me. Brett has lots of friends that he's known forever, whereas I have none.

I decided a long time ago that it was safer *not* to have friends, because I can never be honest with them. Maybe I can cut myself some slack now, because Brett and I have been together for over four years and I haven't slipped up once.

Not once. Perhaps it's time to stop worrying that I'll give myself away.

Because I'm an excellent liar.

CHAPTER FOUR

'**D**o we have to go?' Brett scoops up a spoonful of muesli and pushes it into his mouth. He's not at all happy about our impending dinner with Fen and Darius tonight and has moaned about it ever since I told him about it. I fight down the urge to snap at him.

'You might enjoy it,' I say, with a calmness I don't feel. 'Fen is lovely and I'm sure Darius is too, from what she's told me about him. We should make an effort to get on with our neighbours.'

'Why?' Brett asks, through a mouthful of muesli. 'We're not going to be living here forever, so why bother? I don't want random people talking to me and getting on my nerves every time I step outside the house. Besides, we have lots of friends already. It's not as if we need any more because we never have time to see the ones we have.'

No, Brett, *you* have lots of friends; I don't. Your public school educated friends and their snooty girlfriends scarcely bother to speak to me when we see them. I have absolutely nothing in common with any of them because their trust fund upbringings don't gel with my *orphaned at eleven years old and brought up by an aging relative* background.

I don't say any of this, obviously.

'Darius has his own company. Imports and exports,' I say, taking a bite of the buttery toast that I've looked forward to all week. I never eat breakfast on weekdays and this is a treat for me, but now, it tastes as if I'm eating cardboard. 'You always say it's useful to have a wide network of friends because you never know what the future holds. They could be useful.'

Brett grunts. I've just repeated the exact words to him that he always quotes to me so he can't argue.

'I might need a new job if Barron doesn't get off my fucking back,' Brett spits the words out. 'The stupid old bastard is disrupting all of my plans.'

Now we're getting to the real reason for his bad mood.

'Why is he being so awkward?'

'Awkward?' Brett tosses his spoon into his breakfast bowl and milk splashes over the table. He doesn't even notice. 'He's being a complete bastard lately, and he's got it in for me. Ever since that prick, Davis, started, he's favoured him over me. He does it all the time. God knows why. Yesterday, Davis even had the gall to imply that he'd been told he was going to get the next promotion instead of me.'

Brett has been boiling about this all week to the extent that since Tuesday, we've not even discussed why I'm not yet pregnant. All he's gone on about is Barron and Davis. He was certain that he'd be moving up a level in the next round of promotions, but now he's less sure.

'Davis is just trying to wind you up,' I say in a soothing tone. 'Ignore him and don't rise to it. You know that you're next in line. Barron has always told you that. He has his moods, but he always comes good in the end. You're always saying how he likes to make everyone suffer a bit before he moves them up.'

Brett pushes his chair back and stands up.

'It's easy for you to tell me to ignore it; you don't have to get out there and earn the money to pay for everything. Barron's being weird with me, I can tell. It's different this time. He's being odd. There's something going on that I don't know about. Every time I turn around, Davis is in Barron's office, sucking up to him and laughing at his crap jokes. Rumours are circulating that they'll cut bonuses this year, even though everyone was expecting a bumper year a few weeks ago. I *need* that bonus. If I don't get what I'm expecting, we're in the shit.'

I bite my lip and look up at Brett, unsure what to say that will placate him. Last year, his bonus was over half a million and he was certain that he'd get much more this year. His nostrils flare, and he stares down at me and then storms across the kitchen to the sink. He leans on the worktop and stares out of the window over the back garden. I get up and go and stand behind him and wrap my arms around his waist, laying my head against his back. He makes no attempt to return my embrace, and I can feel every part of him is rigid with anger. His mobile phone rings from the table and after a moment, he pushes my arms down and walks over and picks it up.

'Hi, mate.'

He stands and listens for a moment and then slips his hand into the pocket of his trousers and walks out into the hall. I listen to his one-sided conversation and marvel that he now sounds completely normal and happy, his bad mood gone. Or maybe he saves it just for me. After several minutes, he ends the call and comes back into the kitchen.

'That was Charlie. He's got a game booked, and he's been let down. Wants to know if I'll make up the numbers.'

He wants to play golf.

I hide my disappointment and paste a smile on my face.

'Today?'

'Yeah, tee off at nine-thirty. You don't mind, do you?'

I mind a lot. He's been at work all week and by the time he gets home, we have dinner and go to bed early because he's worn out from his job. Now he wants to spend the day playing golf with his friends while I'll be stuck here on my own. I thought we could go out somewhere, spend the day together. One phone call from a mate and I'm forgotten.'

When I don't immediately answer, Brett walks over and pulls me into his arms.

'Sorry, Nat, for being such a grumpy bastard.'

'That's okay.' I wrap my arms around him and breathe in the smell of the herby shampoo he's used to wash his hair. 'I know how demanding your job is.'

'It is, but I shouldn't take it out on you. Sorry. I know we've hardly seen each other all week, but I'll make it up to you. And I promise I'll be on my best behaviour tonight to meet the neighbours. Scout's honour.'

He kisses and nuzzles my neck, and I giggle.

'And who knows, when we get home maybe we can resume our baby-making.'

I hold him tightly and then kiss him before he can say any more. He pulls me closer and his hands are beginning to roam when we're interrupted by his phone pinging and vibrating in his pocket.

'Shit.' Brett releases me and pulls his phone out and glances at it. 'Charlie's waiting outside. I'd better get a move on.' He dashes out into the hallway and I hear him opening the closet door. I walk to the kitchen doorway and watch him rummaging around until he finds his golf shoes and jacket.

'You're sure you don't mind, Nat?' He shrugs

his coat on and then kneels down and slips his trainers on. When he stands up, he looks at me for a moment, awaiting my approval, golf shoes in one hand, mobile phone in the other. I'm hardly going to say no, not that it would make any difference; he'd still go, I'd just look like a misery for trying to stop him.

'Of course not,' I say. 'Enjoy yourself, get some fresh air, forget about work. It'll do you good.'

'You're too good to me.' He strides towards me and kisses me hurriedly on the cheek and then squeezes past me into the kitchen.

'I'll be back in plenty of time for your dinner thing,' he calls, as he opens the door into the garage. I don't have time to answer before the door closes with a bang and he's gone.

I look at the clock; five-past-nine.

It's going to be a long day.

I clear the breakfast things away and load up the dishwasher. I stand and stare around the kitchen before going into the utility room and taking the vacuum cleaner out of the cupboard. I set about vacuuming the already clean ground floor and by the time I've finished, it's still only a quarter-to-ten. I contemplate doing the rest of the house but abandon the idea because it absolutely does not need doing. I fill the kettle with water and put it on to boil to make myself a cup of tea and stand and stare at it. I flick the switch again to turn it off.

I don't need tea; I need to do something. Something other than pointless housework and drinking cups of tea and wandering from room to room feeling bored. I think about it for a few moments and then go out into the hallway and up the stairs and into my dressing room. I open several of the wardrobe doors until I find what I'm looking for. I take out my oldest, comfiest trainers, a hoodie, and a pair of jogging pants and then close the door.

I'm going out for a run.

* * *

I feel slightly self-conscious as I emerge from our driveway onto the street and jog gently along. Although there's no need because there's no one around. Not a soul. I head towards the park entrance and as I go, I gradually increase my speed. The air is fresh because it's still quite early, but the sky is clear and the sun is bright in the sky. I run through the park and past an empty bandstand and then take the path that encircles the lake. My feet crunch on the gravel as I run and my breathing grows heavier with the unaccustomed exercise.

It's a good feeling; it makes me feel alive.

I used to run a lot before I met Brett. Running would clear my head and I could pound the streets for hours and hours in the evenings after work. Sometimes, I'd run late at night or in the early hours of the morning. If I couldn't sleep and my thoughts were crowding in on me, I'd run. I never felt afraid even though I was alone, and it was dark, because I was confident that I could outrun any attacker. Now that I think about it, I see it was probably a foolish thing to do, and I never told Brett because I knew he would be horrified. As I run, I wonder why I stopped running, but of course I know why. It was because I met Brett.

When we first got together, we spent every spare moment with each other, so I couldn't fit in my running anymore. To make up for the loss of running, I did what all of our—Brett's—friends did, which was to join a very expensive gym. I reasoned that an hours' worth of weights and classes would compensate for the hours of running that I used to do. I'd go religiously every weekday, as Brett did, but my heart wasn't really in it. I found it boring and had to force myself to go, which I never had to do with running. When my membership came up for renewal shortly after we moved here, I let it lapse. My intention had been to find a gym closer to our new home, but I haven't bothered. Brett still goes to the same gym in London that he's always used because it's close to his offices and he works out before he starts work.

I haven't done any exercise at all since we moved to our new house, but now I'm running, I can feel how much I've missed it. My calf muscles are aching as I start my second lap of the lake, but it's a good feeling. I urge myself on. My muscles cramp and I have to stop to stretch it out; hardly surprising, as I didn't warm up at all. I won't make the same mistake next time.

Next time.

I'm going to run every day, or at least every day that Brett is at work, because it will give me something to do. Also, I'll be able to stop starving myself if I exercise. I never used to diet or put on weight when I ran or went to the gym, but since I stopped, I've had to watch everything I eat. I'll be a lot happier eating normally, because being hungry all the time is bloody miserable.

I decide not to do a third lap of the lake because I've already overdone it. I'm going to ache so much tomorrow. I head towards the park entrance and jog slowly back home.

I let myself into the house and go straight through to the kitchen and get myself a glass of water and drink it down in one go. Running is thirsty work and the next time I go, I'll take a bottle with me. I glance at the kitchen clock to see that it's half-past-twelve; I've been out for over two hours.

I untie my trainers and ease my feet out of them. My socks are damp with sweat and as I push my hair from my forehead, I can feel I've been sweating there, too. I pad upstairs and into our ensuite and strip all of my clothes off and drop them into the laundry basket. I step into the shower and stand underneath the hot running water and soap myself and wash my hair.

By the time I'm dressed in fresh clothes and I've dried my hair, I'm starting to feel tired from all my exertions but it's a *good* feeling. I'm hungry too, and I'm going to make myself some lunch and actually enjoy eating it without feeling guilty or fretting that I'm going to pile on the pounds. Maybe I'll take a nap afterwards because I want to be fresh for tonight. I can put the TV on and put my feet up. I'm suddenly feeling much more positive about life and appreciative of what I have. We have nice new neighbours—although I haven't met Darius yet, I'm sure he'll be just as nice as Fen— who will hopefully become friends. I've rekindled my love of running, so I have something to fill my days with and who knows, perhaps, soon, I'll feel confident enough to try to get pregnant for real.

Which means I can stop lying to Brett.

I jog down the stairs, pick up the post from the doormat and take it with me into the kitchen. I quickly sort through it, tossing the pizza leaflets and coupons into a pile for the recycling bin. I put aside the one remaining letter that's addressed to Brett. It looks like a bill, so I'll let him have the pleasure of opening it. I pull open the cupboard door to the recycling bins to throw in the leaflets when I realise that there's an envelope caught up between them. I catch hold of the corner of it and my breath catches in my throat as I pull out a lavender coloured envelope. The name and address are written in blue ink in large, loopy handwriting. I put the envelope on the worktop and stare at it, all thoughts of making lunch, forgotten.

Thank God Brett's not here, because he would

have seen it; he would have heard the letterbox clang and would have picked up the post. I immediately laugh out loud at that thought, because it wouldn't matter if he saw it. The name on the letter isn't the name I have now, and Brett would have no idea it was meant for me. He'd assume it was for one of the previous owners of this house. I'm aware that laughing out loud when I'm on my own makes me sound slightly crazy.

I am.

Because I thought that moving out of London would put a stop to this.

It hasn't and I have to face facts.

I'll never be free.

I thought that I'd escaped. Each day that has gone by, I've become more convinced that I'm safe. It was such a long time ago and I can't understand why it's happening now. I know now that it's never going to go away and I have to face the truth; I'll never be free and I'll always be looking over my shoulder.

I could be found out at any moment.

But I can't tell Brett the truth now; it would be the end of us. There have been too many lies and now it's too late. Lies have been the foundation of my life since I met Brett. Why didn't I tell him the truth when we first got together?

Because it would have been the end of us then, too, and I didn't want to lose him. Foolishly, I thought, no, hoped, that there was no possibility of him ever finding out about my past.

I want to throw the letter away and pretend it doesn't exist. The urge is so strong that I open the bin in readiness and suspend the letter over it.

But I can't.

I did that before and it hasn't worked.

I'm going to have to open it.

CHAPTER FIVE

'You look so hot in that dress, Nat. Why don't you tell them we're ill and we'll stay home?' Brett nuzzles my neck and slides his hands down my legs. I force myself to laugh as I gently pull his hands away.

'We can't cancel now because we're late already.'

'Spoilsport. I have to spend the evening with the boring neighbours when I'd much rather be in bed with my wife.' Brett pulls a face and I laugh again. He's obviously had a few drinks at the nineteenth hole, which explains why he didn't get home until seven o'clock. But he's in a good mood and I'm relieved. Despite feeling disappointed that he didn't spend the day with me, I can see that a round of golf has lifted his spirits. It's taken his mind off his work problems. I hate to see him so down about his job when I know how much it means to him.

If I hadn't received that letter, I'd be feeling good, too.

There is absolutely no point in dwelling on it now and ruining the entire evening, so I push the thought away. I've spent the entire afternoon obsessing over it, and I refuse to think about it anymore. I've achieved nothing by my worst-case scenario thinking except to depress myself thoroughly.

And I still haven't even had the guts to open the envelope and see what's inside.

'Come on,' I say, slipping my coat on. 'Let's go before they think we're not coming.'

Brett takes hold of my shoulders and stares at me.

'Honestly, Nat, I know I've been a pain all week, but I do love you, you know.'

I put my hand on his face and then rub my hand over his hair, which is still wet from the shower.

'I know you do, and I love you, too.'

We share a moment and then I drop my hand and break the spell and march out into the kitchen. I pick up the bottle of wine and the flowers for Fen from the worktop and then go back down the hallway.

'You take the wine.' I give the bottle to Brett. 'And I'll take the flowers.'

Brett looks down at the label, angling the bottle so he can read it. He frowns.

'Hey, this is one of my good ones,' he protests. 'Haven't we got a cheap one we can take?'

'We're taking that one,' I say, as I pull open the front door. 'Because you don't want them to think we're cheapskates, do you?'

* * *

Whilst Fen is in the kitchen organising dessert, I take a sip of wine and sneak a look across the dining table at Brett and Darius. They're deep in what looks like serious conversation until Darius suddenly breaks into a roaring laugh. Brett joins in and I can see from his face that he's thoroughly enjoying himself.

I'm relieved; I hadn't met Darius before today and when I walked into their lounge and saw him; the sheer presence of him shocked me. Brett is tall, but Darius is even taller. At least six-foot-five, he has a thick thatch of black, curly hair and a bushy beard, and the obviously expensive shirt he was wearing failed to disguise his huge shoulders and well-muscled arms. When he turned from the window to greet us, glass of wine in hand, he looked intimidating and almost frightening until he smiled, and then his entire face changed. Flashing a brilliant-white smile at us, he boomed *hello* and strode across the room. He took my hand in his huge paw and leaned in and kissed me gently on both cheeks. He then turned to Brett and gave him a handshake that turned into a man-hug, throwing one of his enormous arms around him. Brett couldn't conceal his shock and Darius must have seen this as he gave a big laugh and said we must forgive him as he hugs everyone.

That was the other surprise; I assumed that like Fen, Darius wouldn't be English, that he'd be from Estonia, the same as her. No, Darius is English through and through and after he'd had quite a few glasses of wine, underneath his perfect vowels, I could detect the slightest trace of a cockney accent. I don't blame him for covering up his beginnings because I've done the same myself. People judge on first appearances and, to some, an accent is not acceptable. Darius and I are alike, I think; I speak very differently now to the way I spoke as a child. It's the reason I usually limit myself to two glasses of wine; the way I speak isn't natural to me and aitches slip after too much alcohol.

Thinking about my past reminds me of the letter and I'm only prevented from descending into a pit of depression by the return of Fen. She comes into the dining room carrying an enormous glass bowl filled with trifle. She places it on the table and then, with a smile, returns to the kitchen. Unlike our house, as well as a vast kitchen with dining and lounge space, they also have a formal dining room. The table we're sitting at could seat eight people with room to spare. I wonder if they entertain a lot because Fen seems very at ease with cooking and the meal she served, an Estonian version of Beef Bourguignon, was delicious.

Fen returns holding a huge jug, which she places in the centre of the table before settling into her seat next to me.

'They like each other,' she says, with a wink, looking at Brett and Darius. 'I'm so pleased that we're all going to be friends.'

'They're getting on like a house on fire,' I say.

'You English have such funny sayings.' Fen laughs.

I laugh with her and I'll admit that I'm relieved that they appear to be getting on so well. Fen and I are already well on the way to becoming firm friends and that would still have been the case, whether Brett and Darius hit it off or not, but the two of them liking each other makes it even better. If only I didn't have the shadow of the letter and everything that it means hanging over me.

'Are you okay?' Fen is looking at me with concern.

'Yes, I'm fine,' I say, after a moment, remembering to smile again.

'You know, I'm an excellent listener.' Fen puts her hand on my arm, her fingers warm through the net sleeve of my dress. 'And I never tell. What goes in here.' She points at her ears. 'Never comes out here.' She points to her mouth.

She holds my gaze for a moment and the urge to tell all is overwhelming. What a release it would be to unburden myself with everything that I've kept secret for so many years. If Brett and Darius weren't sitting opposite, I would be so tempted to tell her everything. I feel tears well behind my eyes and I press my lips together to stifle my emotions.

Darius's booming voice echoes around the room and I stretch my lips upwards, determined not to do anything to draw attention to myself.

'My favourite dessert!' Darius throws his arms wide. 'Brett! You must have some of Fen's magical dessert. You will taste nothing better than this, I promise you.' He picks up his dessert bowl and waves it in the air. Fen stands up and takes it from him, picks up the serving spoon and ladles trifle into his bowl. Feeling foolish at nearly breaking down in front of Fen, I get up from the table and excuse myself to go to the bathroom. After walking down the hallway to their cloakroom, I go inside and close and lock the door. I put the seat down on the toilet and sit down and try to stop my hands from shaking. I can't believe that I came so close to blurting it all out; if Brett and Darius hadn't been there, I have a horrible feeling that I would have told Fen everything.

What is wrong with me?

I've kept my secret for twenty years; is a kind word from a new friend all it takes for me to destroy everything that I've worked so hard for? Could I betray Brett by telling a near stranger everything that I've kept from him since the day we met?

As I wash my hands, I study my reflection in the mirror above the basin. My skin is pale and I pinch my cheeks to inject colour into them. It doesn't work. I should have used more blusher.

Pull yourself together.

I smile at myself but look ghastly and ghost-like. Taking a deep breath, I attempt another smile, and it's better this time. I remind myself that I have a wonderful life with a man I love.

I will not allow anything to spoil it.

One letter is not going to ruin the life I have so carefully constructed.

All I have to do is keep calm and think before I do anything rash.

I take another deep breath and smooth down my dress before unlocking the door and leaving the cloakroom. As I reach the dining-room door, I paste a pleasant expression on my face and go in and sit down. As I settle in my seat, Fen looks at me with a questioning look on her face and I smile at her.

'I can't wait to try your dessert, Fen,' I say. 'Can I help myself?'

'Of course, but you'd better hurry before the boys eat it all.'

Darius guffaws from across the table and Brett joins in. Their dessert dishes are empty and Darius is opening another bottle of wine.

'We've already had second helpings,' Darius says, expertly pulling the cork from the bottle. 'Which is why Fen always makes enough for twenty people.'

I laugh as I ladle the trifle into my bowl and pour cream over the top.

'I'm afraid it's very calorific,' Fen says with a grimace. 'But you and I don't need to watch our weight.'

Smiling, I agree with her, and I push my spoon into the liquor soaked fruit.

Yet another lie.

* * *

It was past one o'clock by the time we left Fen and Darius's house and as we staggered across the road; I thought what a wonderful evening it had been. After dessert, Darius and Brett disappeared into the garden to smoke cigars and have a brandy. Fen looked disapprovingly at Darius, but he smiled at her and said that surely he could celebrate his new friendship with a cigar? She said that they were mad because if the cigars didn't kill them, the cold would. Darius laughed uproariously and said that real men didn't feel the cold.

I helped Fen carry the dishes through to the kitchen, and she made no mention of my emotional moment earlier in the evening, which I was grateful for. As she loaded the dishwasher and we chatted, we could smell the aroma of cigars from the garden as the large folding doors that stretch across the back of the kitchen were open slightly. Their voices drifted through the open doorway and I'm sure that I heard Brett talking about Barron, which surprised me, because Brett is normally quite reserved with people he doesn't know well.

But Brett was quite drunk, and Darius was too.

Alcohol loosens the tongue, because I'd only had a couple of glasses of wine and I felt an urge to confess all to Fen, too.

When we left them, Brett made them promise they would come to dinner at our house and he and Darius repeated their man-hug and their warmth with each other seemed genuine.

Once we got in, we went straight upstairs to our bedroom. As Brett got undressed, throwing his clothes on the floor, he told me how glad he was that we'd met them, and what a great couple they were. Darius was a great guy, he announced, and generous, too, because the second bottle of wine he opened cost three hundred pounds a bottle. Three hundred pounds a bottle, he kept repeating, as if it meant something. He said it made the bottle we took with us look cheap.

Brett knows his wine; he prides himself on being a bit of a wine buff and he said that he couldn't believe it when he saw the bottle, but what most impressed him was that they opened it for us to drink. Or Brett, rather. Darius said he had a case that he saved for sharing with special friends, and I know Brett felt very flattered by his remark.

After Brett got undressed, he flopped into bed and said he'd be waiting for me when I came back. By the time I came out of the ensuite, having brushed my teeth and undressed, Brett was sound asleep and snoring.

I pulled the duvet over him, picked up his

clothes from the floor, and turned out the light. I took his clothes into the ensuite and threw them in the laundry basket and then went into the dressing room. There was no point putting it off any longer; the contents of that letter might keep me awake, but the not knowing was going to make sleep impossible, anyway. I pulled open the wardrobe door and took the letter out of the pocket of my fur coat.

I stared at it for a moment and then, with shaking fingers, I slipped my finger underneath the flap and ripped it open.

There was a single piece of paper inside and I pulled it out and unfolded it. I stared down at the handwritten words and acknowledged that I know the handwriting well. Even after all these years, it's hardly changed. There is only one line of writing with a mobile phone number written underneath.

I take a deep breath, and let the words sink in.

I just want to talk to you.

CHAPTER SIX

We spent yesterday loafing around the house after our evening with Fen and Darius. Brett had a stinking hangover and wasn't in a fit state to do anything or go anywhere. He looked so ill I actually felt sorry for him. It wasn't a bad day, though; we watched trash TV and ate takeaway and Brett had more or less recovered by the time we went to bed.

He kept complaining that he couldn't understand why he felt so bad, because he was sure that he hadn't drunk *that* much. I laughed and reminded him that Darius had opened three bottles of wine and I'd only drunk two glasses and I was pretty sure Fen only had one. And what about the brandy when they were out in the garden smoking their cigars? He groaned and clamped his hand over his mouth at the mention of the cigar, and said the thought of it made him want to throw up. But despite him feeling so rough, and my worry over the letter, it was a good day; a day that I relished because we spent it together. It was a kind of limbo day, because I knew that at some point soon, I would have to make a decision about the letter.

Although deep down, I already knew what I was going to have to do; I have to tell Brett the truth.

I should have told him yesterday and got it over with, but I made excuses to myself because I didn't want to ruin everything. I wanted one last day of normality before I blow our world apart. One more day of Brett not looking at me as if I'm some sort of monster.

Tomorrow, I promised myself, as I went to sleep, I'd definitely tell him tomorrow.

It was my first thought on waking this morning and I knew it would be going around in my brain on a loop, so, after Brett left for work, I set about cleaning the house. Not that there actually was anything *to* clean; we're both tidy people and I'd vacuumed it on Saturday, so there wasn't even any dirt to pick up, but I needed to keep myself occupied.

Once I'd finished and put the vacuum cleaner away, I put on my trainers and went out for a run. I took the same route that I took on Friday and I ran for nearly two hours. Despite my aching legs, I felt as if I could run forever because when I'm running; I don't have to think. It was the same when I was cleaning; if I'm focused on an activity, I can stop my mind from going into a constant nightmare of imagining the worst.

After I've showered and changed into fresh clothes, I do what I've been avoiding doing all weekend.

I send a message to the mobile number on the letter.

Give me some time. I type, *I'll be in touch soon.*

I sign it with the name that I was born with; the name I was known by until I was old enough to legally change it.

Holly.

I don't know why I used my old name because it's not as if the person who wrote the letter doesn't know my new name.

The person.

Why do I keep referring to her as *the person*? Her name is Wendy. We were best friends a long time ago and despite changing my name and trying to erase my past, somehow, she's been able to find me. What I can't understand is why; why has it taken her so long? Why now? It doesn't make any sense. I stare at the screen and watch the message go and then see the two ticks that show it's been read. It's done.

I should feel better for having done it.

But I don't; because now I have to tell Brett the truth.

I've promised myself that I'd tell him tonight and that's what I'm going to do. No excuses. It's time to face the consequences. I've planned a nice dinner for when he comes home and after we've eaten, I'm going to sit him down and tell him the truth about my past.

The condemned woman ate a hearty meal.

Engrossed in mindless chopping and preparing everything for dinner, it's only when I glance at the clock that I realise it's gone half-past-six and Brett hasn't rung me. He always rings me just before he gets on his train, *always*. The call goes straight to voicemail when I ring him, but I don't leave a message and hang up. I finish prepping dinner and try not to worry. I remind myself that he'll be on the train on his way home and the mobile signal will be bad.

That's why he hasn't answered.

But why didn't he ring me? He *always* rings me.

My mind veers off in crazy directions; he's had an accident, he's fallen onto the tracks, he's having an affair and is going to leave me for someone else.

Or maybe he's found out about me, somehow, and is never coming back. I've missed my chance. I should have told him the truth when we met and now it's too late because he can't forgive me.

As if it will help, I start to pace up and down the kitchen. It doesn't, of course, but I can't seem to make myself sit still. By the time he walks into the house at twenty-past-eight, I'm nearly hysterical with worry and am about to start ringing around the hospitals to see if he's been admitted after an accident. The minute I hear the door open, I rush out into the hallway to see Brett closing the front door. He turns and stares at me, his face expressionless, and drops his briefcase onto the floor, where it lands with a thud before falling onto its side.

'Where have you been?' I shriek. 'I've been so worried. I thought something had happened to you. Why didn't you ring me?'

'I've been at work. Where do you think I've been?' He shrugs his coat off and drops it on top of his briefcase.

I can tell immediately that he's been drinking; he has that glassy-eyed look that he always gets. Oh God, he *knows*. Somehow, he knows about me. Somehow, he's found out.

'What's wrong?' I ask, forcing myself to calm down, as if acting normal will make everything okay. 'Why are you so late?'

'What are you, my mother?' he snaps, walking through into the lounge and heading straight to the sideboard. He pulls the door open, takes out a bottle of whisky and a tumbler and pours a hefty measure into the glass.

'What's happened, Brett?'

He doesn't answer but puts the glass to his lips, tips his head back and swallows the contents in one go. He puts the glass down and swiftly pours another.

'Brett, please, what's wrong? You're frightening me.'

He picks up the glass and studies it for a moment, drinks it in one mouthful, and then slams the glass down onto the sideboard again. The noise makes me jump and I push down a rising feeling of panic.

'Oh dear, what a fucking shame. Natalie's frightened. We can't have that, can we?'

I stare at him; stunned. I have no idea what to say. This isn't the Brett I know. This cold, nasty man in front of me bears no resemblance to the man I love.

I walk over to him. 'Brett, tell me what's wrong. Please, talk to me. Maybe I can help.' I put my arms out to hug him, but he pushes me away.

'Stop fussing around me for a start. That'll help. I've had a bad day, okay?' He sloshes yet more whisky into the glass, spilling it over the sideboard, then picks it up and walks over to the armchair and flops down heavily into it. 'Look, I'm not in the mood to talk. Just leave me alone. It's work stuff, you wouldn't understand.'

'Try me.'

He knocks back the whisky and then immediately gets up and pours himself another.

'There's no point. It's a fucking mess and you HAVE NO IDEA, so just leave me the fuck alone.' Glass in hand, he paces to the bay window and stares out into the darkness.

'Why don't you come and eat something? I've cooked dinner. It might make you feel better if you eat.'

Brett turns and stares at me, a look so dark that for a moment, I'm almost afraid of my husband. When the silence feels as if it can't stretch any further, he bursts into loud laughter. It's mocking, derisory laughter, and not in the slightest bit funny. I turn and go out to the kitchen and wonder what to do. I don't know what to say to him, but I know that something is badly wrong.

What is it he won't tell me?

I start to pace again, trying to decide what to do. I've just decided to go back into the lounge when I hear the front door opening and then the bang of it being slammed shut. I hurry into the hallway to see that Brett's coat is gone, his briefcase still lying on its side on the floor.

He's gone out.

But where?

* * *

I never told Brett that I've been lying to him since the day we met because how could I when he's barely speaking to me?

It's now Thursday, and he's in no better mood than he was on Monday.

He won't tell me what's wrong, but I know that it's nothing to do with my past. It's something that's happened at work.

I don't know where he went to on Monday night when he left the house. He hasn't told me and I haven't asked him. He came home in the early hours of the morning, reeking of whisky and cigars. I pretended to be asleep as he crashed around the bedroom, getting undressed and throwing his clothes everywhere. I made no sound when he flopped into bed next to me and fell into a deep and noisy sleep, snoring for most of the night.

When I awoke the next morning at just after six o'clock, his space in the bed next to me was empty. I got up and went downstairs, but he wasn't there. I assumed he'd gone into work early.

He never rang me from the station on his way home that night, nor has he on any of the nights since. He wasn't late, though, and he wasn't drunk. Neither of us made any mention of the night before and when I asked him again what was wrong, he looked at me coldly and told me *not to keep on*. We've barely spoken all week. So many times, I've opened my mouth to ask him what the matter is, only to close it again.

I feel as if I'm living with a stranger.

I've decided I'm going to tell him the truth about myself tonight, because I can't go on like this. Telling him can't make things any worse, because he's barely speaking to me, anyway. He's never been like this before, never. I might as well just tell him and get it over with.

Fen wanted to meet for coffee yesterday but I couldn't face it; I just didn't have it in me to sit and pretend that everything was just fine when it's not. I know that if she showed the slightest bit of concern or kindness to me, I'd blurt everything out, and I don't want to be disloyal to Brett. So, I lied to her; because that's my go to behaviour. I messaged her I had a dreadful cold and wasn't feeling great. She messaged back and asked if there was anything she could do, and that made me feel even worse.

I couldn't stay in the house, though, because I would have gone insane trapped in these four walls all day. But I couldn't go out because if she spotted me running in the street, she'd know I was lying. Then I remembered that there was a gate at the end of our back garden where I could get out without being seen. We never use it, but I know when we viewed the house that the estate agent enthused about there being a 'greenbelt' at the back of the house. I put my running gear on and, after a battle with the rusty bolt on the gate, I let myself out. The 'greenbelt' is just a small patch of rough grass dividing our house from the next street, but that's estate agents for you. I ran across it and then pounded around the surrounding streets until I couldn't run anymore. I was breathless and sweating by the time I returned home. Today I ran too, because running is the only thing that's getting me through the days. I'm going to use the *having a cold* excuse for Saturday night, because Fen and Darius are supposed to be coming here for dinner and there's no way that's going to happen with Brett in his current mood.

Last Saturday night seems like a lifetime ago, a *different* life, a different husband.

I don't bother preparing any dinner for tonight. Brett won't have any appetite at all after he's learned the truth about me. I won't prolong it. I'll be confessing all the minute he gets home. Perhaps it's too late, anyway. Maybe he's already fallen out of love with me. Maybe he's treating me with such coldness because he no longer loves me. He hasn't so much as put his arm around me since Sunday and I still can't quite believe that he's changed so quickly. It's as if he's two people; if it wasn't such a ridiculous thought, I could believe another person had replaced Brett.

The hands of the clock crawl around to six o'clock and, of course, Brett doesn't ring.

Our new normal.

I pace around the kitchen, which is my new normal, until I hear his key in the door. He doesn't call out *hello* and I stop myself from dashing out into the hallway to greet him.

Like I always used to.

I'll let him get in and take his coat off and get settled in the lounge before I attempt to speak to him. I wonder if he will drink again. He didn't drink last night, but who knows, in this weird new life of ours, nothing is predictable.

I take a deep breath and walk in to see that he's not drinking, but is sitting slumped in the armchair, staring into space. He seems unaware that I'm in the room. I use the opportunity to look at him. I mean, properly look at him. He's looked angry all week, but now he looks exhausted. Defeated. There are dark shadows underneath his eyes, but the rest of his skin is pale, so very pale. He doesn't have his usual healthy glow. I feel a rush of love for him; what is it that's making him this way?

I cross the room to stand in front of him, aware that whatever's bothering him, I'm about to make it a lot worse.

'Brett?' My voice emerges in a whisper, and I repeat myself, louder this time. 'Brett?'

He looks up at me and for a moment I wonder if he's been crying, or that he's about to cry. He looks in absolute despair. I kneel next to the chair and put my arms across his chest, fully expecting him to push me away.

But he doesn't.

'Brett, tell me, please, what's wrong, what's going on?'

He takes hold of my hand and grips it, and I relish the feel of his fingers on my skin after what feels like months, not days, of no contact.

'I'm sorry,' he whispers. 'So sorry. I've been such a pig.' He turns to face me and his voice is hoarse and he sounds defeated.

'What is it?'

'I'm so sorry. I've taken it out on you and none of it is your fault. None of it. I'm a horrible, vile bastard and I don't deserve you.'

'It's okay, it doesn't matter. Just tell me what's wrong. Please. I can help. I can't bear to see you like this.'

He takes a deep, shuddering breath.

'I'm going to lose my job, Nat.'

'What?'

'I'm done for, Nat. We're going to lose everything.'

CHAPTER SEVEN

Brett jumps up, walks over to the sideboard, and picks up the bottle of whisky. I stand up and watch him.

'Brett, don't shut me out again.'

'I'm not.' He shakes his head. 'I promise, I'm not. I just need a drink. Do you want one?'

I'm about to say *no, drinking won't help,* but stop myself. Saying that won't help either, will it?

'Just a small one for me.' I hate whisky, but I want to join in with him; I don't need to actually drink it. I don't want to fuss around getting a bottle of wine from the kitchen cooler and risk Brett clamming up again.

Taking a tumbler from the cupboard, he pours in a measure of whisky and hands it to me. I take it and when he sits back down in the armchair; I settle down on the sofa opposite him. He gulps down a mouthful of whisky and begins to speak.

'Do you remember I told you that Barron's been off with me for a while? Well, it's got a whole lot worse. He's positively gunning for me. If I still have a job at the end of the month, I'll be surprised.' He takes another swig of whisky and his mouth turns down at the corners as he swallows; it looks painful, as if he's having trouble getting it down. He stares into space and I wait for him to speak. I have to let him tell me in his own time and not badger him for details.

I've only met Barron a handful of times and each of those occasions was at a company dinner. In his late fifties, with a potbelly and a florid complexion, I couldn't help but take an instant dislike to him. Snobbish and chauvinistic, I only tolerated his sexist jokes and constant put downs about *the fairer sex,* as he referred to women, because he's Brett's boss. Even as I pretended to find him funny and laughed at his pathetic jokes, I felt disgusted with myself. I consoled myself with the fact that I had no choice, because to do anything other than that would have been to Brett's detriment. I knew I had to suck it up and be pleasant to Barron if Brett wanted to get on in his career. I had to tolerate him once in a blue moon, so I could make myself do that. But I still hated having to sit there and listen to him because he is everything I hate in a man.

Brett had warned me, the first time I met Barron, that I'd detest him on sight. He told me he was an aging, sexist dinosaur, but he had all the right connections and had been to the right schools and university so was in an unassailable position of power. Barron's a fully paid-up member of the old boy network and whilst Brett doesn't like it, that's the way things are. We have to play the game because to do anything else will severely impact Brett's career. One of the other fund manager's girlfriends had taken exception to Barron's sexist remarks and made the mistake of taking him to task for it. Barron didn't like it one little bit, and it didn't end well for her boyfriend; he eventually left the company when he realised that his promotion prospects had sunk to zero because of her response to Barron.

I take a sip of whisky. It burns my mouth and I try not to gag. Why am I even drinking it?

'I told you about Davis, didn't I?'

'The new guy?'

'Yeah. He's a complete prick. The day he started, I couldn't understand why Barron took him on, because we didn't *need* another fund manager. All the accounts were assigned and everything was ticking along nicely. I'd inherited the Grantby account after Tom left, which meant that I was ninety-nine-point-nine percent certain to get a top bonus this year. That's why I felt so confident about moving here, because Barron pretty much said I was next up for senior manager and, along with the bonus, I'd be all set. We'd be *made*. In his own way, he promised me. He never actually comes out and says the words, but I've known him long enough to know how he works. He's always come through before and I had no reason to think that this time would be any different.'

I wait while he takes another swig of whisky.

'So. Anyway. Davis and I disliked each other on sight. The bloke's a creep and so full of himself, it's unbelievable. I didn't care because I don't have to interact with him on a daily basis. We have our own accounts and don't need to have much contact with each other. Which was fine until Barron started being off with me. Davis was always in Barron's office sucking up to him and then it got that every morning, first thing, he'd be in there for half-an-hour chatting to him, like they were best buddies or something. Then I noticed that every time *I* went into Barron's office, he was always too busy to see me. *Come back later*, he'd say, not even looking up from his desk. I felt as if I was the new guy, not Davis.'

'Couldn't you ask Barron what was wrong? You've always got on well with him, can't you just have it out with him?'

Brett laughs without humour. 'I got on with him because I sucked up to him and laughed at his jokes, like everyone else. It was one way traffic. You *never* question Barron, you just take what he says and put up with it. He won't tolerate being questioned about anything. I've been lucky. He promoted me because I was good at my job. I was his favourite, but now Davis is here, he's the new favourite and I'm out. On Monday, I found out why.'

He stands up and walks over to the sideboard and refills his glass again, and I wish he'd slow down; he's drinking too much.

'Barron's got a spoilt brat of a daughter and Davis is her new fiancé.'

'Oh.'

'Yeah, exactly.'

'How did you find out?'

'Davis told me. He enjoyed telling me, too. Says he's getting the next promotion and I might as well do myself a favour and leave now.'

'What a nerve!' I say. 'It won't happen, though, because he has to prove that he can do the job. He can't get by on being the boss's son-in-law alone. When he's not getting the business in and making Barron any money, he'll soon tire of him.'

'He doesn't need to get any new business. He doesn't have to prove himself like everyone else.' Brett laughs bitterly. 'Barron gave him the Grantby account, so he's made. He called me into his office and told me I wasn't performing well enough and he was giving the account to Davis. It doesn't leave me with much because I had to off-load most of my other accounts when I took Grantby on. I told Barron this, and he said to stop whining and bring in some new accounts.'

'But that's so unfair! There must be something you can do, it's blatant favouritism. Can't you go to HR or something?'

Brett shakes his head.

'I could, but it won't do any good. They'd investigate and Barron would wriggle out of it and I'd be left with a massive black mark against me. He'll tell them I'm underperforming, and they won't be able to disprove it, so I'll end up on a performance plan and I'll be managed out. My name will be tainted forever. It'll follow me. If I leave the company and go elsewhere, I'll have to declare I've made a complaint against my manager and no one will touch me with a barge pole if I do that. I'll never get another job, Nat. Barron's a vindictive bastard and he knows *everyone*.'

'But why? I get he wants his son-in-law to be to do well, but he always thought a lot of you.'

'No, he didn't. I was in the right place at the right time, and now I'm not. I'm in the way. Davis has been putting the poison in, too. He's been telling tales about all the guys in the department to make himself look good. That's why he kept their relationship quiet at first, so he could find out what everyone really thought of Barron and use it against us.'

'You think he's been doing that? Reporting what you've said behind Barron's back?'

Brett shakes his head.

'I *never* talk about Barron in a detrimental way because I don't trust anyone. No, Davis just makes it up, says stuff to make me look bad and him look good. I know he's done it because he's told me.'

'He told you?' I ask, incredulously.

'Yeah, and he loved telling me, too. Thinks he's so clever. Says it's only going to get worse for me, so I'd better look for another job and jump before I'm pushed.'

'Because you're a threat?'

'Yep. He's frightened I'll bring in some new accounts and make him look bad. I'm the one that can make his performance look crap and he wants me out of the way.'

'What are you going to do?'

'I don't know. I don't think there's anything I can do. It's all I've thought about all week and it's driving me mad. I'm so sorry I've been so horrible to you. It's not your fault.'

'It's okay,' I say. 'That doesn't matter now. Just talk to me and don't bottle it up and shut me out. We could have been helping each other instead of living like strangers for the past few days. We could have talked about it when you came home on Monday instead of you storming out and getting drunk.'

I feel bad as soon as I've spoken because I sound accusatory and whiny, making it about me when it's not. But I can't help that I'm hurt.

Brett gets up and comes over to the sofa, and sits down next to me.

'I can't tell you how sorry I am. I'll make it up to you, I promise. I'll never be like that again.' He puts his arms around me and I relax into his embrace, the tension from the last few days leaving my body. I wrap my arms around him and hold him tightly.

'Where did you go?' I ask. 'On Monday? I thought you were going to stay out all night.'

'I wasn't far away,' he murmurs into my hair.

'I was across the road with Darius; he plied me with brandy while I bored him to death with my moaning.'

I'm stunned; he told Darius, someone he's met only once, all about it whilst I was at home going out of my mind. I stay silent, not trusting myself to speak.

'Hey.' Brett releases his hold on me and sits back and looks at me. 'Let's go out for dinner. I'll get changed and we can go to that little Italian place we went to on your birthday. I want to make it up to you. Say sorry for the way I've been this week. What do you say?'

'You want to go out?

'Yeah, I do. Treat ourselves while we still can.'

'Okay,' I say, even though I'm not the slightest bit hungry.

'Right. You put a nice dress on and I'll get changed. I'll ring for a cab, then we can both have a drink.'

I get up from the sofa and head towards the hallway.

'Do you think we need to book?' Brett says from behind me. 'Maybe I'll give them a ring and check.'

'Probably best to,' I say, as I head up the stairs. My voice sounds normal, but inside I'm in pieces. Why did he tell Darius and not me? Why did he tell someone he barely knows when he couldn't talk to his own wife?

Which is when I remember.

How close I came to confiding everything to Fen

on Saturday night, when I felt so low that the urge to confess was nearly overwhelming. I can hardly blame Brett for confiding in Darius when I was ready to tell a woman I've only just met a secret that I've kept for the last twenty years. The secret that I was intent on telling Brett this evening but is now the furthest thing from my mind.

❋ ❋ ❋

I thought I wasn't hungry and that I'd be unable to eat a thing, but I was wrong. I devoured my Fettuccini Alfredo as if I hadn't eaten for a week. When I thought about it, I'd eaten little since Monday, mostly just pushing the food around my plate every evening as I sat opposite Brett at our kitchen table. The lump in my throat was a physical obstacle to getting food down.

Brett seemed *almost* his normal self; he insisted he wasn't going to give in to Davis and give his notice in. Instead, he'd work hard on bringing in more accounts, which would make Barron happy because he was greedy, if nothing else. He'd brought in new accounts before, when he started working there, and that's what had made him Barron's favourite. I think Brett was trying to convince himself. I went along with it, although from what he's told me, I think that he's going to have to leave. I didn't want to spoil the evening because it was so nice to have the old Brett back instead of the cold stranger I'd lived with all week.

By the time we got home, we were both giggly from the bottle of wine that we'd shared. We tumbled into bed, forgetting all thoughts of Brett's job worries. As we pulled off each other's clothes and made love for the first time in a week, I knew no matter what happened with his job, we'd get through it.

I'm drifting off to sleep when I awake with a jolt; with everything that has happened since Brett came home, I've forgotten to take my pill. I listen to the sound of Brett's steady breathing and then slip out of bed and go into the dressing room. I pull the door almost closed and then put the light on before going to the wardrobe and taking my pills out of my coat pocket. The letter falls out with it and I stuff it back in, unwilling to even think about it tonight. It can wait. I pop the pill out of the blister pack and swallow it. I'm about to put the packet back when Brett's voice startles me. Suddenly clumsy, the packet falls from my fingers and onto the floor in slow motion.

'What are you doing, Nat?' he asks.

I turn and look at him in shock. The packet is lying on the carpet in full view, and Brett is staring right at it. He can see exactly what I'm doing. He looks bewildered and confused, and I see comprehension start to dawn in his eyes.

'Let's go back into the bedroom,' I say, ignoring the packet on the floor and walking towards him.

'Why?' He backs away from me, as if he's afraid I might touch him. 'Tell me why you're taking the pill when we're supposed to be trying for a baby?'

'I will,' I say. 'But it's a long story and it'll take a while. I have a lot to tell you.'

CHAPTER EIGHT

'**N**ot much longer.'

Wendy bites her lip and I see the tears well in her eyes.

'It'll be alright,' I say. 'And you'll be here tonight with me. You'll be safe.'

We're sitting on the bed in my bedroom. The mattress is lumpy, cold and hard beneath us, and I can feel a broken spring poking into my leg. We haven't taken our coats off because it's freezing; nearly as cold as it is outside. The heating is broken and getting it fixed isn't a priority in our house. Booze comes first. First, second, and third. Booze comes before everything. It's the only thing that Dad cares about. The only way our house will ever be warm again is if Dad has a win at the bookies and I persuade him to fix the heating before he spends it all at the pub or puts it on a horse. I'd have to get him in a good mood and turn on the tears to get him to do it, and even then, I'd be lucky if he actually agreed. Anyway, I've got used to washing in freezing water now and truthfully, I don't wash at the weekends because it's not like I'm going to see anyone.

Except for Wendy.

Wendy's my best friend and she's the only person in the whole world who knows the truth about my dad and my life. And I'm the only one who knows the truth about hers.

We're like sisters. I'm like Wendy's big sister, even though she's only three months younger than me. I feel a lot older than her. She's only little, dinky, my mum used to call her. I know Wendy looks up to me and listens to me as if I know what I'm talking about. I like that because no one else bothers with me.

I wish we were proper sisters in a proper family.

'I'm cold,' Wendy says, rubbing her hands together.

'Me too. You've brought the sleeping bag, haven't you?'

'Yeah, it's in my backpack. We can sleep in it tonight under your duvet. It'll be warmer.'

Wendy's staying over at my house tonight. She told her mum that we're having pizza, watching a film and having a sleepover. She's lying; Dad doesn't even know that she's here because we came in by the back door and came straight upstairs. He was in the lounge with the door shut and the television on and some tinnies. Once he's drunk his tinnies, he'll go out to the pub. By the time he gets home tonight it'll be late and he won't know she's asleep in my bedroom because it's not as if he'll bother looking. He mostly sleeps downstairs on the sofa and rarely makes it upstairs to bed. If he's awake in the morning and sees us, I'll tell him I asked him if she could stay over and he said it was okay. He won't argue, because he's drunk or hungover all the time and can't ever remember what he's said or done.

Wendy pulls her legs up and wraps her arms around them and hugs them to her body.

'You can go to sleep properly tonight,' I say. 'Close your eyes and everything and once we're cuddled up in the sleeping bag, it'll be nice and warm.'

'Be better than the bathroom floor.' Wendy shudders and then starts to cry. I put my arms around her and hold her tightly.

'I'm so scared,' she says through sobs.

'You don't have to be.' I clench my fists behind her back and try to breathe slowly. Getting angry won't help Wendy.

Wendy doesn't like shouting.

'Your mum will defo be at work?'

'Yeah,' she murmurs. 'She's always gone by half-six and he goes out as soon as she's gone, even though he pretends he's looking after me. He never comes back before ten o'clock.'

That gives us loads of time. Wendy's mum works night shifts at the laundry and once she's gone to work, there's no chance of her coming home. We'll wait until eight o'clock because it'll be properly dark and Dad will have gone to the pub by then. He doesn't come home before pub kicking out time. Even if he did, he wouldn't know I wasn't here because he never bothers checking on me anyway.

'Will it work?' Wendy asks. 'It is going to work, isn't it, Hol? 'Cos I don't know what I'm going to do if it

doesn't.'

'It's going to work,' I say firmly. 'And then you won't be able to live in your house anymore and you and your mum will have to stay with your nan. You know your nan hates his guts, so she won't let him stay. You'll be safe then. He won't be able to get to you.'

Wendy starts to cry again and I rub her back, the same way that Mum used to when I was little. When she did it, I always felt better. I push the thought away. I try not to think about Mum if I can help it because it makes me cry and I miss her so badly. Dad never used to drink so much when she was here. I wish she wasn't dead.

'This time tomorrow,' I say. 'It'll all be over and you'll be free.'

'I wish we didn't have to do it,' Wendy says, in a small voice.

'So do I.'

We have to, though.

Because her mum's new boyfriend, Griff, won't leave Wendy alone. He was alright at first. He gave Wendy sweets and let her watch films with him and her mum like a proper family and sometimes they even went to the pictures and the speedway together. They had takeaways and everything. I thought Wendy was really lucky, and I was jealous, too, because Dad doesn't take any notice of me; I don't think he remembers that I'm here most of the time.

When Griff started touching Wendy, stroking her arm and the back of her neck and stuff, she didn't really like it, but she thought that was what dads did.

I told her my dad didn't do that, but he did used to cuddle me and kiss me goodnight when Mum was alive. But that was a long time ago. So even though he wasn't her proper dad, Wendy said she could put up with it to be in a real family.

But it got so much worse.

When he first came into her bedroom after her mum had gone to work, Wendy didn't understand what he wanted until he got into bed with her.

He said she had to be nice to him.

She told him she was always nice to him and he laughed and she knew, then, what was going to happen.

She didn't bother shouting or screaming because there was no one to hear her. She knew that what he did to her wasn't what dads were supposed to do, and she shut her eyes and pretended she was somewhere else. He made her bleed. The next night, she never went to bed but went into the bathroom and locked herself in. She stayed there all night and dragged a chair out of her bedroom and pushed it underneath the door handle as well, just to make sure that he couldn't get the door open. She's been doing the same thing every night for over a week; every night that her mum's been at work. She lies on the bathroom floor wrapped in the duvet from her bed instead of sleeping in her bedroom. She doesn't sleep though, because she's too frightened. He rattles the door and talks to her, pretends he's nice and promises to buy her stuff if she opens the door. When she won't open it, he starts shouting and says horrible things to her; tells her what he'll do to her when he gets the door open.

It's only when she hears her mum coming in the front door from work in the morning that she opens the door and comes out. She knows she's safe when her mum's home.

Yesterday, Griff unscrewed the lock and took it off the bathroom door. He threw it away and told her mum that it was broken and that he was going to get a new one. He was looking at Wendy all the time he was saying it and her mum didn't even notice. Wendy said her mum was chuffed that Griff was doing some DIY. We know he won't ever get a new lock and now Wendy's got nowhere to hide.

'I wish we didn't have to do it, Hol.'

'I do, too. Are you sure you can't tell your mum or your nan? Tell them what he's been doing to you?' We've talked about this loads and it always comes back to the same thing; she can't.

Wendy shudders.

'I can't. Mum won't believe me 'cos she loves him. She's always saying what a great step-dad he is and how lucky we are to have him. He's always nice to me in front of her. And she likes it 'cos he always has money for fags and stuff. And I can't tell my nan 'cos Mum will never forgive me, she'll keep on and on and hate me forever and say I've ruined everything. Anyway, even if I told them, it wouldn't help, because he said he'll come back and kill me if I do. Or worse. Said he'll kidnap me and no one will ever find me and all of his mates can have a go on me before he chops me up into little pieces.'

She sobs and I wrap my arms around her and she clings to me.

'We're doing it and it'll work.' *I try to make my voice sound all grown up and teacher-like.* 'Let's not talk about him anymore. I hate him and one day you can get your own back on him somehow, I don't know how. For now, we just have to make sure he can't stay in the house anymore.'

I hear a bang from downstairs and know that it's the sound of the front door shutting. Dad has gone to the pub. I look at my alarm clock and see that it's a quarter to seven.

'Right, come on, let's go downstairs and get the stuff ready. The sooner it's done, the sooner we can come back and watch telly and pretend it's not happening.'

We get up from the bed and go downstairs. There's no need to get our shoes on as we never took them off and we already have our coats on. We're going to feel even colder when we get outside because it's windy and cold.

You won't feel the benefit.

That's what Mum used to say; she said if you don't take your coat off straightaway when you get home from school, you'll feel even colder when you go out again. I keep thinking about Mum, even more than I usually do. It's because I feel guilty about what we're going to do.

It's a bad thing.

I wonder if Mum is watching me from heaven.

She'd be so disappointed in me.

If she was still here, I wouldn't have to do it. Mum would have sorted everything out, she'd have gone round to Wendy's house and talked to her mum and Griff would be gone. Or she'd have gone to the police. She loved Wendy as much as I do. Wendy could have come and lived with us and we could have been proper sisters if Mum was here.

I head towards the kitchen and push the thought of Mum away. Again. But not before I tell her I love her and I'm sorry and that I'm only doing a bad thing because of a very bad man.

I go into the kitchen, and Wendy follows. There are empty pizza boxes all over the worktops and dirty plates and dishes piled in the sink. I feel my feet sticking to the lino as I walk over to the sink and I feel ashamed. Mum would hate this house if she could see it now.

It used to be so clean and tidy and warm.

I make a promise to myself and Mum that after we've done this, I'm going to clean the house. Just because Dad doesn't care how we live, it doesn't mean that I don't either. I know how to use the hoover and how to wash up, even if there is no hot water. I can boil the kettle.

I pull open the cupboard door underneath the sink and reach into the back, and pull out the metal can. Wendy has a plastic carrier bag ready that she brought from home and I lower the can inside. Even though I twisted the top of it tightly shut, I can smell the petrol that's inside. I found the can at the back of Dad's shed; he's got everything in there but he never uses any of it anymore so he won't notice it's missing. I go over to the kitchen drawer and open it and rummage through the jumble of tea-towels until I find the box of matches. They're longer than normal matches, so won't burn down so quickly. I tuck them into the pocket of my coat.

'Let's go.' I look at Wendy.

She nods and I see her Adam's apple move as she swallows. It looks like it hurts, like she's swallowing something big and hard.

We walk out to the hallway and I turn off the light before opening the front door.

That way, no one will see us leave the house.

We step outside and quietly close the front door behind us and begin the walk to Wendy's house.

✻ ✻ ✻

We start off walking fast to warm up and to get there quickly, but as we get closer, we both slow down.

Because once we're there, we have to actually do what we've been planning and talking about. I was the one who thought of the plan. I'm the one who's persuaded Wendy that it's a good idea.

We're going to set fire to Wendy's house.

No one will get hurt, except for the house. It's just a house and the council will rehouse Wendy and her mum, but it'll take a while because everyone has to wait ages and go on the waiting list to get a house. The house next door to Wendy's is empty. There used to be a family living there, but the man was a bully and his wife and kids moved out to get away from him. A couple of weeks ago, he went, too, though nobody knows where.

So no one will get hurt.

If the house burns down, they won't be able to live in it and Wendy and her mum will have to live with her nan while they wait for a new one. We're hoping that by the time the council finds Wendy and her mum somewhere else, Griff will have got fed up and moved on.

Wendy was frightened when I told her the plan. She said there must be something else we could do.

There isn't; we've thought and thought and there's nothing.

I asked Wendy what she'd do if we don't do this and she looked so sad and said that she didn't know, but she thought she'd be better off dead. I didn't like the way she said that, because she sounded like she didn't care if she died.

What if she killed herself? People do that, don't they? When they can't see a way out.

'Tell me what to do,' Wendy whispers, as we reach the street before hers.

'Go the back way.' I push her past the end of her street towards the back alley. 'Remember, we're going down the alley so no one will see us. Put your hood up.'

She flips her hood over her head, and I do the same.

We hurry down the alley until we reach her house and I open the rusty gate that's falling off its hinges and we walk up the overgrown path to the back of the house. There are no lights on in the house because all *the windows are dark. We stop before we reach the back door and crouch down behind the coal bunker.*

'Are you ready?' I ask. 'You remember what we're going to do?'

I see Wendy's head nod in the gloom and we both look up at the house in the darkness. Wendy is staring at her bedroom window and I see her eyes glistening. She's going to cry. I stand up and grab hold of her hand to pull her with me. She stands up but doesn't move.

'Come on,' I urge.

'I can't,' Wendy sobs. 'I can't.'

CHAPTER NINE

When I finish speaking, there's silence.

We're sitting downstairs in the lounge with only the lamp on the coffee table for illumination. I found it easier to talk in the near darkness because I couldn't bring myself to look at Brett as I told him. I didn't want to see the disgust written on his face. He asked no questions nor interrupted me while I spoke, and I was grateful for that.

'What happened?' he asks.

I take a deep breath and force myself to answer him; the next part is going to be the worst and I have to make myself continue. I don't like to think about it, let alone talk about it.

'Yes. And it was terrifying and much worse than we could have ever imagined. Talking about it was one thing, going through with it was another. Wendy never had to go back to that house, so we achieved that. But we'd made a mistake; a terrible, fatal mistake.'

I pause, but Brett doesn't speak. His eyes never leave my face as I force myself to continue.

'Griff was still there, in the house, fast asleep. He'd finished work early and gone to the pub. One drink had turned into a drinking session and he was sleeping it off in one of the bedrooms.'

'Christ.' Brett's eyes are round. The reality of what I'm telling him is sinking in. 'He was in there?'

'Yes. He died of smoke inhalation. Wendy and I had no idea how to set a fire; we were lucky that we didn't set ourselves ablaze. The initial fire caught rapidly, but it was a damp night and the fire smouldered, rather than burned. The house was more or less intact once the fire brigade had put out the flames, but the smoke was thick, black and choking. According to the coroner, Griff would never have even woken up.'

We sit and neither of us speak and when the silence becomes unbearable, I continue.

'It didn't take very long for the police to put two and two together. They arrested us at my house early the next morning. They had to break down the front door because my father never answered their insistent knocking. He'd passed out on the sofa after a heavy night at the pub. They found us huddled in the sleeping bag in my bedroom. We couldn't have looked more guilty; we still reeked of petrol and, if that wasn't enough, one of Wendy's neighbours had seen us walking along the alley. That was the last time that I ever saw Wendy. It was a condition of our sentencing that we weren't allowed any contact.'

Until now. I don't tell Brett this, because what's the point when we'll no longer be together?

'Why didn't you tell me?' Brett asks. 'When we first got together? You could have told me, then.'

'Why didn't I tell you?' I repeat. 'Because it would have been the end of us the minute I uttered the words. I wanted to be with you. Would you have wanted me if you'd known I was a murderer? You wouldn't. I didn't want you to know that about me; you would have looked at me differently before you ran for the hills. You would have looked at me in exactly the way you're looking at me now.'

There's silence and I know it's only a matter of time before he asks me to leave, but what he says next surprises me.

'What's the reason for you not wanting a baby? Why have you been lying to me about that? If you didn't want a baby, you should have told me. Why lie?'

'I want a baby. I do. But I think a part of me knew that one day you'd find out about me.' I sigh. 'I knew I couldn't live a lie forever and when you found out, that would be it. You'd want nothing more to do with me, and I don't blame you for that. I couldn't let myself get pregnant because if we split up, I didn't want my child to have a broken family and a terrible childhood like mine.'

'You should have told me,' Brett says. 'You should have trusted me enough to tell me the truth. And being brought up by your grandmother, I assume that was a lie, as well?'

'It was. They sent me to a secure unit and then several years later after they judged I was ready to be released, I was put into care. I never settled anywhere, despite being fostered by several couples. My father drank himself to death by the time I was fourteen, so there was no possibility that I could go home. Not that I wanted to. At least I gained an education and got to university. That wouldn't have happened if they'd sent me back to where I came from.'

Brett leans forward, puts his hands on his knees, and I try not to flinch as his eyes search my face.

'So since the day I met you, everything you told me about your childhood and growing up was a lie?'

I make myself look him straight in the eye.

'Yes. And there's not a day that I haven't regretted it. There have been so many times I've longed to tell you. I'm so, so sorry. It's no excuse but I lied because I didn't want to lose you.'

He looks down and we break eye contact and I know that I've lost him. There's no going back from this. We continue talking for hours, Brett asking me question after question about my life in care. I answer his questions with facts. I don't tell him about my loneliness and despair, my lack of family or of any love, because he doesn't need to hear that. I don't deserve any sympathy after all the lies I've told.

The fact that my father never visited me once, I keep to myself.

They placed me in a secure unit while I was assessed and I stayed there for several years. I got used to it but during those first few months after the fire, I was terrified, but I don't tell Brett this, either. I never saw Wendy again, and I was bereft; I'd lost the only person in the world who cared about me. But worse than that, I was afraid for her, scared of what she might do to herself. My questions to the social workers and carers were met with silence when I asked about her. When they asked their questions, I did the same. I refused to speak about the fire; I sat silently and let them assume what they liked, because I knew that confessing or trying to justify what we'd done would make no difference. I didn't know what Wendy had told them. Had she told them about Griff? I didn't think she had because she was so ashamed of what he did to her. She thought she was to blame. I couldn't see her telling anyone, ever.

Griff was an abuser, but would it have made any difference to what happened to us if I'd told the authorities this? I'm not sure; we'd done something terrible, and had to be dealt with. I was fortunate; no one was physically cruel to me and my life was better than it had been for a long time. I no longer had to wear my coat to bed to keep warm. I had clean clothes to wear and regular meals. And although I never made another genuine friend in all of my years in care, or when I went to university, I had many acquaintances. I'd made a new life for myself and become a different person because I so hated the old one.

I tell none of this to Brett, but stick to the facts; how I worked hard at school and went to university and gained a business degree. Everything from that point on in my life was the truth, aside from the fictitious grandmother who'd brought me up passing away just before we met. I have a real grandmother somewhere, or I did. She's most probably dead by now. I won't be trying to find her, my father's mother, because she made no attempt to help in my upbringing when my mother died and had played no part in my life before that. She ignored her son's escape into alcoholism after his thirty-seven-year-old wife died after a brief battle with cancer. My father and her were never close, and she stayed away and pretended not to know what was happening.

I used to blame my father for his neglect and lack of care for me, but I look back now and feel pity for him. He couldn't cope; he'd lost his wife and didn't know what to do. There was no one to help him. I have memories of him before my mother died; happy times when we were a proper family.

He needed help, but he never got it.

Light is filtering through the lounge curtains when Brett stops questioning me. He's very calm and I marvel at his composure; I'm not so sure that

I'd have been so calm if I found out that everything I knew about him was a lie.

'I'm going to get ready for work,' he says, standing up from the chair.

'Work?' I echo. 'You're going to work?'

'Yes. I'm going to take a shower. It's nearly five o'clock. No point in going back to bed now. Besides, I can't stay off today, not with the way things are.'

I stare up at him, trying to read something in his expression, but I can't. *The way things are.* Does he mean me or Barron? I don't ask. He doesn't look at me as he walks away, and I hear him cross the hallway and go upstairs.

I sit, immobile, with no idea what I'm going to do.

* * *

Brett left for work, even earlier than usual, and who can blame him?

He didn't kiss me goodbye, but he *said* goodbye, so that's something, isn't it? It's just one word, but it means he's still speaking to me. He didn't ignore me. I'm trying not to read anything into the fact that he's still speaking to me and hasn't told me to get out. He's in shock and has to process the fact that his wife's a liar. Perhaps when he comes back tonight, he'll tell me to pack my bags and go.

I won't argue. Not because I want to leave, but because he doesn't need me to make it more difficult for him. What's the point in putting up a fight when there's no possibility of winning?

After he's gone, I go upstairs and get into bed and pull the duvet up to my chin. I lie there, exhausted but unable to sleep. Everything is whirling around in my head as I stare wide-eyed at the ceiling.

All I can think about is losing him, and I ask myself if I feel better now he knows about my past.

I should have told him before. I should never have lied to him, but when would have been the right time to tell him? Our first date? No, because we hardly knew each other, and I didn't know we were going to stay together. So when is the right time - the third date, the tenth date? There is no right time and if I'd told him when we first met, does that mean I should have confessed all to every man that I ever went out with?

Should I have told him when we got engaged? The eve of our wedding?

There never was a right time. Each day that went by made it more impossible to tell him the truth. Was the letter from Wendy the catalyst for me finally telling him? Maybe it was; if she'd never contacted me and made me so afraid that Brett would find out, I might have carried on living with all of my lies. Although, I know that in time, the secret would have been too much for me to bear. It was always there in the background, the enormous elephant in the room that was ready to spoil everything, ready to destroy this life that I'd so carefully constructed. I thought I had a new life, but my past was the reason I couldn't allow myself to become pregnant. The fear that I'd be found out and lose my child, as well as Brett, that I'd repeat the mistakes of my father. Taking the pill and making sure that I didn't get pregnant was only a temporary solution, because I couldn't have carried on doing that forever. I think I knew, deep down, that I was going to have to tell him.

When Wendy contacted me, I panicked and saw her as a threat to my happiness, but I've always known the truth; that she would never hurt me or cause me any worry. She was like a sister to me. I was shocked that she'd found me, because if she could find me, my past hadn't been buried at all. It would always be there, waiting to be discovered.

And underneath the panic, I felt relief, relief that Wendy was still alive.

I'm going to message her and arrange to meet.

Soon.

Because I have a sudden longing to know what she's been doing for all these years.

I hope she's had a happy life.

I turn my head and look at the alarm clock on the bedside table; nine-fifteen. I clamber out of bed and pad to the bathroom. I've been lying awake for hours and there's no possibility of sleep. I'm going to shower and dress and go for a run.

Brett knows the worst now.

There's nothing more I can do.

Except wait.

CHAPTER TEN

I open the front door and step outside.

The cold air hits me; it's freezing. The sky is a dull, mottled grey and I remember the radio weatherman's prediction of heavy snow. Pulling the door closed behind me, I slip the key into my pocket and zip it up. I jog down the driveway, through the gate that Brett has left open, and out onto the path. I break into a run, speeding past Fen's house to lessen the likelihood of her seeing me. She must think that I'm avoiding her. If I was thinking straight and my brain wasn't so full of Brett, I would have left by the back gate and avoided the risk of Fen seeing me.

Too late now.

My excitement at meeting Fen and thinking that we might become firm friends seems a lifetime ago. I can't help feeling foolish now at my desperation for us to be friends.

I head towards the park and concentrate on my breathing. In and out, in and out; I repeat the words in my head in time with my breaths, one after the other, leaving no room for any other thoughts to push their way in. As I run through the entrance to the park, I feel a flake of snow flutter onto my face, but I don't stop.

I need to run.

By the time I reach the lake and begin my circuit, one flake of snow has turned into a flurry and they blow into my face, blizzard-like and icy-cold.

I keep on running.

I force myself onwards, and as soon as I've completed one circuit of the lake, I begin another. There's no one else around and a part of me knows I should go home because the snow is getting heavier. The cold has numbed my fingers and the snow has soaked and plastered my hair to my head. My face is numb and devoid of sensation but my ears are so cold they hurt. I relish the pain and keep running as if I can run away from the hand grenade I've just thrown into my life.

The snow is settling as I complete the second lap and the entrance to the park is in view, but I don't want to go home; I don't want to think. Several inches of snow now covers the ground, but I can't seem to make myself stop running. I'm passing the entrance, intent on doing yet another lap of the lake when I slip on the newly laid snow. Arms windmilling, I'm unable to stop myself from falling and I tumble forwards, twisting my ankle. My outstretched hands meet the rough path and one of my wrists bends backwards as I'm unable to stop myself falling. I land heavily on the ground; the impact knocking the breath from me.

I lay still, momentarily stunned; the ground is cold and hard beneath me and I consider staying there. I close my eyes and think how much easier it would be if I never had to get up again.

Let the snow settle on me and bury me and make everything go away.

'Bloody hell, Nat, are you okay?'

The voice is familiar. I hear footsteps growing closer and open my eyes to see the figure of Darius approaching me. He's running and I want to tell him to be careful; not to slip over like me, but the words won't come.

'Here, let me help you up.'

He kneels down beside me and I feel his muscular arms working their way underneath me. He gently lifts me and helps me to my feet.

'Did you knock yourself out?'

His arms are around me, gripping me firmly, and the woolly material of his overcoat is in my face. The heat of his body radiates to mine and there's the hint of a smell of aftershave and minty toothpaste. I have an urge to rest my head on his chest and close my eyes.

'Are you okay?' His eyes search my face and he's too close, much too close.

'I think so,' I manage to say, pulling myself away from him before I make a complete fool of myself.

'You sure? Because you had your eyes shut when you were on the ground, I thought you were unconscious. I think we should get you to a doctor, get you checked over. Can you walk? I can carry you if not, it's not far to our house.'

'No, honestly, I'm fine.' I have no idea if I am.

He turns, his arm around my shoulders, his hand firm on my arm. He guides me along and we walk slowly to the park entrance. My legs seem to be holding me up and I don't feel any pain anywhere.

Just numbness.

I think I'm in shock. I can hear Darius talking to me, but somehow, even though he's right beside me, his voice is getting further away. I glance up at the sky and wonder if it's going to snow forever because the clouds are growing darker and darker.

A humming noise is coming from somewhere and it's getting louder. I look up at Darius in puzzlement and wonder if he can hear it, too. I open my mouth to ask him, but the humming is so loud I can't make myself heard. Day turns to night and as I slide into oblivion, all that's in my mind is that I'll never be warm again.

'I'm fine.'

'You don't look fine.' Fen is studying me with concern. 'You should see a doctor. You could have concussion, or worse.'

'I didn't hit my head at all.' I shake my head to disagree with her and then wish I hadn't. It hurts and feels as if something is loose behind my eyes. I wonder if I did bang it when I fell. 'I twisted my ankle and bent my wrists back, but apart from that, I'm fine. It was my fault for being stupid and running in this weather.'

'Darius said you had your eyes closed when he found you,' Fen insists, not for the first time. 'He's not sure if you knocked yourself out or not.'

'The snow was falling in my eyes,' I lie. 'That's why I closed them. I was just readying myself to get up when he found me.'

She doesn't comment and I can tell she doesn't believe me. I stop myself from trying to convince her because I don't have to; it's my choice whether to see a doctor. I won't be bothering and that's the end of it. I'm sitting on their sofa with a large fleecy blanket wrapped around me. Like an invalid. I don't remember getting to their house at all. I woke up when Fen opened the front door, her hand flying to her mouth in shock. Darius was holding me in his arms, having carried me from the park when I'd fainted.

'I'm okay now,' I say, after a while. 'It was the shock, and the cold, and I'm just getting over an awful cold.' I give a little cough to reinforce my lie about having been ill. It was only two days ago that I refused Fen's offer of coffee by pretending to be ill, and I don't want to hurt her feelings.

I shiver underneath the blanket and clamp my teeth together to stop them from chattering. Fen and Darius have been extremely kind, making me cups of tea and settling me next to the fire to warm me up. Fen wanted to give me dry clothes to change into, but I refused. I just want to go home.

'Eat your sandwich.' Fen pushes the plate with the sandwich closer to me. 'And I'll get you another cup of tea with lots of sugar in it for the shock.'

I don't want the sandwich or sweet tea; I just want Brett to forgive me.

I force myself to smile and pick up the sandwich and take a bite. It tastes like cardboard in my mouth, but I chew it until it's mashed up enough to swallow. I can feel the beginnings of a headache, but I don't ask Fen if she has any paracetamol because she'll insist that I see a doctor. I don't have the energy to argue with her again. A part of me knows that if Darius hadn't found me, I would still be lying in the park now. I could have concussion but no way am I sitting in A and E for hours to find out. Once I'm home and warm again, I'll be okay.

Fen takes my cup from the coffee table and goes out into the hallway. Darius is out there because I can hear his voice, but not well enough to hear what he's saying. There's something about the way he's speaking that makes me think he's agitated; an urgency in his words. I listen and wonder who he's talking to and then decide I don't care. Fen returns with another cup of tea and closes the door behind her. She smiles and places the cup in front of me on the coffee table. The ticking of the clock on the mantelpiece replaces the sound of Darius's voice. I look at the hands on the clock and am shocked to see that it's almost three o'clock.

How long was I running for?

I thought I ran around the lake twice, but maybe that's not right; it must have been more than that. It wasn't snowing when I left the house, but by the time I fell, a thick blanket of snow covered the ground.

I shove the sandwich into my mouth and take another bite; once I've eaten this and drunk the tea, I'm going home. They've been very kind, but I just want to be alone. I want a hot shower and to sleep forever. I feel exhausted.

I look up when the lounge door opens again. It's not Darius.

It's Brett.

*　*　*

Brett closes the front door behind us and, without taking my trainers off, I walk straight up the stairs and into our bedroom. I go into the bathroom and drop Fen's fleecy blanket into the laundry basket, then close the door. I strip off my damp clothes and trainers, reach in and turn the shower to hot, and step underneath the water. I close my eyes and turn my face upwards and the hot water cascades over me. For the first time in hours, I begin to feel warm.

I shampoo my hair and rinse it and then wash myself all over. By the time I step out of the shower, I feel almost human again. I go into the dressing room and take fresh underwear, fleecy joggers and a hoodie from the chest of drawers and put them on. Despite the hot shower, my feet still feel cold, so I pull on fluffy socks. I towel dry my hair and consider drying it with the hairdryer, but simply don't have the energy.

There's no sound from downstairs and I wonder what Brett is doing. Maybe he's not here anymore, maybe he's gone out or gone back to work. When he appeared at Fen and Darius's house, I felt elated when I saw him - until I saw his expression. His face was closed and unforgiving, and I wondered why he'd bothered to come and get me. I guessed Darius had rung him and told him about my accident. I should have thought of this and told Darius not to contact him. I curse myself for my stupidity, because now I've made things even worse. With the way work is at the moment, the last thing he needed was to have to leave the office early.

When Brett came in, I got up from the sofa and thanked Fen and Darius for their kindness, and we left. Brett sounded normal when he spoke to Fen and Darius and for a moment, I had hope that perhaps we'd be okay. As we walked across the street to our house, he put his arm around my waist to support me and my heart soared. We were going to get over this. But as soon as we arrived at the front door, and he unlocked it, he dropped his arm. He stood silently and waited while I stepped inside, and I knew then that he was only putting on a show to save embarrassment. The only reason he'd put his arm around me was because they were watching.

Now that I'm dressed, what am I going to do?

I walk onto the landing and stand for a moment at the top of the stairs, listening.

Nothing.

I don't think Brett's here. He must have gone back to work, although it can hardly be worth it now. I could go downstairs and find out for sure, but I don't. I turn and go back into the bedroom and climb into bed. I pull the duvet over my head and close my eyes. My eyelids are so heavy and my head hurts and gradually, the weight of the duvet and the warmth of the bed comforts me. I pretend to myself that everything is normal and Brett is sleeping next to me, and somehow, I fall asleep.

I dream that I'm running through the snow and someone is calling my name. It's Brett; he's calling my name, he's no longer angry, and he's the old Brett, the Brett *before*. In my dream, I smile, and then the snow is getting heavier, so heavy that everything is shaking, the world is shaking. I don't want to wake up from this wonderful dream, but I can't stay asleep any longer. As I open my eyes, I see Brett's face in front of me. He's leaning over the bed and shaking my arm.

I stare up at him.

'Nat, are you okay?'

'No,' I say, bursting into tears.

'Oh, Nat.' He sits down on the side of the bed,

wrapping his arms around me and pulling me up to his chest. 'I'm so sorry. I've been such a fucking idiot.'

'You've nothing to say sorry for,' I whisper, wondering if I'm still dreaming.

'I have, Nat. You didn't feel you could tell me the truth, and that's my fault for being such a snob and having this stupid life plan.'

I want to pinch myself to make sure that I'm not dreaming, and I say this to Brett. He laughs ruefully.

'You're not dreaming and I'm admitting I'm a pompous prick, Nat, but it won't happen again, so make the most of it.'

'I should have told you, Brett, I should have told you long ago, but I convinced myself I was doing the right thing. I was ashamed, too. I didn't want you to know.'

'You were just a child, eleven-years-old, for God's sake. I feel sick when I think about what you've been through.' He pulls me closer and holds me tightly.

'You don't hate me?' I whisper.

'Hate you?' He sits back and studies my face. 'How could I ever hate you? You tried to help your friend. She was being abused, and you helped her. Someone should have been helping *you*. I could cry when I think about what you've been through.'

All the years that I've kept my secret, all the anguish that I've caused myself and I could have told him, I *should* have told him.

I should have trusted him.

'I'm sorry I dragged you out of work. What did Barron say when you left early? Will it cause you even more trouble?'

'Barron?' Brett laughs. 'He didn't say anything, because I never went to work.'

'What? You never stay off work. Never.'

'I know, but I did today.'

He tells me then how when he left the house, he walked around the streets until the local coffee shop opened. He was their first customer, and he snagged himself a table in the corner, opened his laptop and pretended he was working. There was nowhere else to go. Brett hates people who work in coffee shops because it's pretentious and selfish, hogging a table for hours on end, but he's now one of them. When the waitress brought him his first cup of coffee, he told her his wi-fi was down at home. He asked her if it was okay if he stayed for a while and she said it was fine. He then ordered another coffee and let that one go cold, too. He ordered a slap-up breakfast he didn't eat, and countless cups of coffee he didn't drink, to lessen his guilt. He thinks they made more money out of him than they did out of all the other customers put together.

I was shocked he never went to work. Brett could see my shock and told me not to feel bad because the way things are, it will make no difference. He's resigned to losing his job. And work wasn't the reason he took the day off. He needed time to take in what I'd told him, time to think about us.

Us.

There's still an *us* and for that I am so grateful.

CHAPTER ELEVEN

I wave Brett off at the front door, fifties' housewife style. The heavy snow that fell on Friday has almost gone. The only remaining clue it snowed at all are small clumps of grubby snow clinging onto the edges of the grass verges and the tops of the rooftops.

When Brett is no longer in sight, I close the front door and go back into the kitchen. I settle myself at the table and resume eating my toast, still unable to believe quite how well the weekend has gone.

We're going to be okay; we *are* okay.

I no longer have to lie to him and fear him finding out about me. I've even told him about Wendy, how she wrote to me and how frightened I was that the truth would come out and ruin my life. He says I should meet up with her, catch up after all these years.

I will.

Perhaps I'll message her to arrange something.

Things have changed between Brett and me, and I'm still adjusting to the new me; the new us. We've promised to be more open with each other, to share our feelings instead of dealing with everything on our own. I thought we already did this, but realistically, we didn't, because there was always a part of me I held back. I could never be honest whilst I was lying about my past. And although Brett talked about work a lot, the successes and the high stakes and the excitement of getting his bonus, he never really shared how he *felt* about it. He only ever told me about the highs and never the lows; which is the reason he found it so hard to talk about Barron and Davis. He's promised to be more honest and tell me the bad as well as the good. He's always had this thing where he wants to be the very best at what he does and to be seen to be successful. A lot of what's going on at work has been eating away at him and he's bottled it up. He's always felt that if he's not super successful at his job, he's a failure.

It's what his father did, and Brett has continued in the same way because that's what he thought he should do. That's the outlook they brought him up with. His father was a successful, high-flying barrister and when Brett was growing up, he was never aware of him ever having any sort of setback or failure. His view of his father was as a brilliant barrister on a one-way trajectory to the pinnacle of his profession. If there were any failures, and there must have been, neither Brett nor his mother were aware of them. That may have worked for his parents' marriage—and it did, because they're still together now—but it's not going to work for us. I don't think it's healthy for Brett to shoulder all the stress alone.

The biggest decision that we've made, and made together, is that we've scrapped the life plan. It's gone, and it's never coming back. Brett made his life plan when he left university and he did it on the advice of his father. His father was of the opinion that Brett needed to know exactly where he was going in life and should set his sights on the future. It's a very different mindset from mine. Aside from knowing that I never wanted to return to the life I had as a child, I had only a vague idea of what I wanted from life when I left university. A job that I enjoyed with a decent income was my ambition, and that was it. Everything else was down to chance, because who can plan a life when there are so many variables?

Not Brett and me, as we're finding out.

So, the life plan is gone for good. I've told Brett that I don't care one bit if we never have a big house or a top of the range car as long as we have each other. I was happy with our London flat before we moved here and if we lose this house, so be it. Life doesn't begin and end at Minerva Avenue.

Starting a family is on hold for the moment,

too, because Brett needs to know what's happening with his job before we make any major life decisions. We're both young and have plenty of time to start a family. The other thing we've decided is that I might go back to work for a while, if I can find something suitable. I used to enjoy my job as a sales representative for a pharmaceutical company and it was only the immense amount of travelling involved that made me decide to leave. I'm going to look for something different, a job without any travelling. I have a good business degree and I should use it. As well as giving me something to do, the income will help when Brett leaves Byersons.

He's accepted that he has no future there and is going to leave. Aside from the fact that once Barron has decided someone is surplus to requirements, they're swiftly managed out of the company, Brett doesn't want to stay there. We know that he's going to have to take a pay cut by going elsewhere; Byersons are the top payers and the annual bonus is unmatched by any of the other companies in their sector of the market. Finding and starting a new job isn't something that happens quickly. Realistically, it's going to take at least three months because that's the minimum time a company takes to advertise, interview, and find the right person. It'll most likely take longer than that. Brett's going to wait a few days and then tell Barron he's leaving and give in his notice. He can then start applying for jobs elsewhere. He won't tell prospective employers that he's working his notice because they'll view that suspiciously. They'd assume that he's been forced to resign because of poor performance and then there's no way Brett will get offered a position in their company. Unless Barron blabs to his chums, there's no way that anyone will know Brett's already given his notice. We're just keeping our fingers crossed he can find a job quickly; he's going to put out feelers to his contacts in other companies to see if there are any opportunities.

This is all dependent on Barron not being vindictive and managing Brett out of the company, regardless of him giving notice. It is, Brett says, a possibility. The good thing is that all being well, Brett will serve out his three months' notice at home as it's company policy to put all leavers on gardening leave.

So our life is going to be different, but it's going to be better.

* * *

I knock at the door and wait. The brass door knocker is in the shape of a lion's head and I'm surprised I never noticed it before. It's huge and impressive. I try to remember whether we used it when we came to dinner and come to the conclusion that we didn't, we pressed the bell.

I'm assuming Fen is at home because her car is parked in the driveway, but she could easily have walked somewhere, so maybe she's not. An enormous bouquet of flowers and a box of handmade chocolates are in my arms as a *thank you* gift for their kindness on Friday. I bought them from the local florists on the other side of the park this morning on the way back from my run. I only did two laps of the lake today; I'm easing back in gently. I had to walk home with the flowers and chocolates as I was afraid the jogging up and down would batter the flowers and make the petals drop off.

Fen and Darius were supposed to be coming to us for dinner on Saturday night, but we cancelled. Brett told them I was still recovering from my fall, even though I was fine after a couple of paracetamol and a good night's sleep, so it was a bit of a white lie, but we didn't feel like entertaining. We wanted the weekend on our own because we had a lot to talk about. I felt mean for cancelling, but Brett called over to their house and told them on Saturday morning and they were sympathetic and completely understood. They offered to cook us dinner and bring it over for us. How sweet was that? Brett politely declined, but promised them we'd sort out another date soon, maybe next weekend or the weekend after. Brett seems much more relaxed now that he's decided to leave Byersons and we're both feeling very positive about the future.

We have each other.

As I wait, I think how lucky we are to have found

such nice people right across the street from us. It would be a shame to move if finances require it, but we could keep in touch with Fen and Darius. The distinct lack of neighbourliness highlights their friendliness even more in this street; I haven't spoken to any of the other people here, aside from the snooty woman I took a parcel in for. I've seen people getting into and out of their cars, but not one of them has called out *hello*. Neither have I. Minerva Avenue has the reputation of being one of the best streets in the area, but it's not exactly friendly here. It's very much like London; we lived in our flat for three years and I can count on the fingers of one hand the number of times I spoke to a neighbour.

We were lucky to get this house for the asking price because it pretty much never happens. Having already sold the London flat, we were in the right place at the right time and completely proceedable. It astounded Darius when Brett told him; they paid twenty-thousand over the asking price for theirs and Darius thought *they'd* got a bargain.

There's no sign of Fen answering the door, so I rap the knocker twice more. No response; she must be out. I debate leaving the bouquet and chocolates on the porch. The only thing stopping me is that there's no card with the gift, so she won't know they're from me.

I'll come back later.

I turn to leave and have stepped off the porch

when I hear something. Is it voices? I'm not sure. Maybe Fen is in and she didn't hear me knocking. Maybe the television is on. I shuffle around the gravel path in front of the lounge bay window and peer through the slats in the venetian blinds. I see movement and move closer to the window to see Fen and Darius standing in front of the fireplace. I raise my hand to tap on the window and then stop and clamp it over my mouth in shock, unable to believe what I'm seeing.

They're not talking to each other as I assumed at first glance; Darius is towering over Fen and has his hand around her throat. His face is inches from hers as he speaks to her, his mouth twisted into an ugly sneer. Fen's arms are hanging loose by her side, like a rag-doll, and she's making no attempt to fight back. I can't hear what he's saying, but Fen looks terrified.

I stand immobile, my mouth suddenly dry and my heart pounding.

Darius's hand moves up to Fen's face and I see him grip her chin with his huge fingers. I catch my breath as I watch Fen's eyes grow wide with fear as he squeezes her face. Without warning, he suddenly releases his grip and pushes her and she stumbles backwards and falls onto the sofa. Darius leans over her and laughs and Fen cringes away from him.

Darius looks nothing like the kind man who picked me up and carried me home from the park.

What the hell should I do?

Darius storms across the room to the doorway and I hurriedly step away from the window and crunch along the gravel path to the front of the porch. I'm halfway down their driveway heading for the gates when I hear their front door open.

'Nat! I thought I heard the bell. How are you? Are you feeling better?'

It's Darius, and he sounds as concerned and charming as he always does. Did he see me through the window? I stand rigidly for a moment before forcing myself to turn around.

'Oh, hi, Darius. I knocked, but I thought you were out.' Can he detect the wobble in my voice? I take a deep breath and continue. 'I have a little something for you and Fen, just a small thank you for your kindness on Friday.'

My legs feel as if they're made from a jelly-like substance as I stand there. There's the merest extra beat of silence before he flashes his perfect smile at me and speaks.

'That's so kind of you, but there was no need.'

There's that smile again. I make myself walk back towards him and hand him the flowers and chocolates. He takes them from me, the box of chocolates looking tiny in his huge hands. I'm suddenly disgusted at myself. I witnessed him attacking Fen mere minutes ago, and now I'm behaving as if nothing has happened.

'Is Fen in?'

'No, she's gone out, I'm afraid.' So smooth. 'But thank you so much for these. You really shouldn't have, though, because we just wanted to help our new friend.'

He looks so sincere that I begin to doubt what I saw.

Am I overreacting? Did I imagine it?

No, I'm not and I didn't. The urge to get away from Darius as quickly as possible is overwhelming. I'm finding it difficult to even talk to him.

'I must go.' I smile, already turning to leave. 'I've left something on the hob.'

The words sound pathetic, even to my own ears. Darius laughs and I turn back and give him a little wave and he flashes that smile at me again. I march down the driveway and through their gateway and tell myself that he's not watching me and that he can't see my legs shaking. I don't convince myself. I recall my impression of him the first time we met; how he looked huge and threatening until he smiled that charming smile.

Maybe my first impression of him was right.

I should do something, because Fen is in that house with that brute of a man and I simpered and smiled at him as if nothing was wrong. To say I feel disgusted with myself is an understatement. I'm finding it impossible to reconcile what I've just witnessed with the man we've become friends with. When he found me in the park, he was so gentle. He was so tender and loving with Fen when we had dinner with them. The way he always smiled at her and called her *darling*, telling us what a wonderful woman she is.

The man is a liar.

I hurry across the road and let myself into the house and close the front door and lock it. The scene of Fen and Darius is playing over and over in my head. The terrified look on Fen's face fixed in my mind.

I know why I locked the door, stupid though it is.

What I witnessed frightened me, and I have to be honest with myself.

I'm afraid of Darius.

CHAPTER TWELVE

I've just closed the front door when I hear my mobile phone ringing. I go into the kitchen and pick it up from the worktop where I left it. Brett's name flashes up on the screen. It's ten past three; he never rings me this early because he'll still be at work and that's a big no-no for him. He says that nowhere is private at work, not even the gents' toilets. Our time for talking is on his way to the station when he's finished for the day.

I try, unsuccessfully, to quell the sense of foreboding that surges up inside me. All thoughts of Fen vanish as I press the button to answer the call.

Something bad has happened.

'Nat.' Brett's voice is quiet, so much so that he's almost whispering. 'I'm in one of the meeting rooms, so I'll have to be quick.'

'What's wrong?' I ask, my heart sinking. Has he changed his mind and given notice today because he can't stand it any longer? We'd agreed that he was going to wait for a few days, maybe a week, but perhaps he just can't take any more of Barron and Davis.

'It's Barron.' I hear a door opening and a voice in the background. Brett speaks, but I can't hear what he's saying. His voice is muffled, as if he's put his hand over the microphone. I take a deep breath and breathe out slowly through my nose to calm myself.

Whatever's happened, we'll deal with it. Together.

'Sorry.' Brett is back, speaking quietly. 'James just came in. I've got rid of him now. Told him I was on a confidential client call. He knows I'm lying, but he can't exactly call me a liar, can he? Especially as he came in here for the same reason as me.' He laughs.

'What's happened?' I ask.

'Barron's dead, Nat. He's dead.'

'Dead?' When? How?'

'Sometime over the weekend, apparently. Details are a bit scant, although there are a million rumours flying around. Shit.'

Brett stops talking, and I hear muffled voices again. I wish whoever is interrupting would go away.

'Fuck's sake.' Brett's back and he sounds exasperated. 'It was Aiden this time. I'm going to have to go; the world and his wife want to get in here and I'll get no peace. We can talk when I get home. I won't bother ringing from the station because we won't have time to talk properly. I just wanted to let you know.'

'Okay, I'll see you later.'

'Love you,' Brett whispers.

'Love you more.' We both laugh and Brett hangs up.

I stare at the screen for a moment and wonder if Barron dying is a good thing for Brett and then feel ashamed for thinking such a thing. A man has died and all I care about is whether it means Brett can keep his job.

What sort of person does that make me?

Human.

Brett will be thinking exactly the same as me because he'd have to be a robot, not to. I could tell from our brief conversation that his mood has lifted. It's not as if I've wished Barron dead and even if I had, it's not as wishing something can make it happen. I can't deny that it could make all the difference to Brett's career prospects. Without his future father-in-law to protect him and further his career, Davis won't do so well. Without Barron, Davis will struggle. Brett is excellent at his job and before Davis came along, he was the top fund manager and well on the road to another promotion.

Don't get your hopes up, my inner pessimistic voice warns.

I can't help it, though.

I recall the occasions that I've met Barron and I wonder what he might have died from. He was overweight, but not massively so. He had a florid complexion and a large stomach that some men get when they get older. He didn't look fit and as if he did any sort of exercise and perhaps he had a heart condition or underlying health problems, who knows. People drop dead every day from illnesses and conditions they are completely unaware of. It must have been something like a heart attack to be so sudden. I try to make myself feel sorry for his family, but don't quite manage it because I've never met any of them and can't visualise them or their grief.

It's no good.

I can't make myself feel sorry; Barron was content to manage Brett out of the company and ruin his career. His life. Did he feel sorry for what he was doing to Brett? No, he didn't. I know Barron's grown-up children and wife will probably feel devastated by his sudden death, but try as I might, I cannot feel sorry about it. I can't stop from thinking that Barron's death could be a lucky accident for us.

It doesn't matter what I think, anyway, because what I think won't change the fact that he's dead. Am I heartless? No; because I'm upset about what I've discovered about Fen and the way Darius is treating her. If I was heartless, I wouldn't care.

I wish there was something I could do to help

her.

I no longer see Darius as a charming, gentle giant, but a brute of a man who beats his wife. I need to talk to Brett and decide what we can do to help Fen. There must be something. I can't pretend not to know what I've witnessed and I feel afraid for her; afraid of what Darius might do to her.

I turn my mobile phone over in my hand and stare at it. It's not even four o'clock yet and the time until Brett arrives home stretches ahead, seeming endless rather than the few hours it actually is. I open WhatsApp and scroll down to Wendy's contact details and stare at her number. Before I can change my mind, I tap her name to open the message screen and begin to type. There's no reason not to meet up with Wendy now; it's time to find out where she's been for all these years and why it's only now that she's contacted me. Time to find out how life has treated her.

Time to deal with the past.

✳ ✳ ✳

'You don't know how he died?'

'Nope,' Brett says. 'Just that it was sudden. Barron wasn't in his office when I got into work this morning and he's always there before me. Always. I noticed Davis wasn't there either, so I guessed something had happened, but had no idea what. Everyone was talking about the two of them not being in and by ten o'clock, there was still no sign of them. That's when the finance director rang me, said that HR would be down to talk to us imminently. Said no more than that. I wondered what the hell was going on; never thought for a minute that Barron was dead.'

Brett's only just got home, and it took all of my willpower not to bombard him with questions the minute he stepped through the door. I waited until he'd got his coat off and then I poured us both a glass of wine and we settled down at the table in the kitchen. The aroma of the lasagne cooking in the oven fills the air.

I can tell that Brett is pleased the director rang him and not one of the other fund managers. I tell him this. He smiles, taking a sip of his wine.

'I have to admit that it made me feel good. I could tell that it pissed off a few people, too, and that made me feel even better. I just hope that I get on with whoever the directors choose to replace Barron. I'm certain they'll promote from within the company; take someone from a smaller department and move them up. There are a few likely candidates and I know all of them, so fingers crossed.'

'It must be a good sign that the director rang you, though, mustn't it? Instead of someone else.'

'I think so. Don't want to get too overconfident, but yeah, it's looking hopeful.'

'So someone from HR came down and told you all that Barron had died?'

'Yeah. He didn't say much, just that he had

some bad news and that Barron had 'passed away suddenly', no more details than that. I assumed Davis wouldn't be in because he's almost family and would look after his wife-to-be. That was it basically; told us if we had any problems, we could contact the finance director directly and that a stand-in for Barron was being arranged.'

'I wonder what happened to him?'

'I'm putting my money on a heart attack. It's got to be something like that to be so sudden. I can't say I'm heartbroken.'

'Brett! That's an awful thing to say, a man's dead.'

He shrugs. 'I'm just being honest. He turned on me, Nat, and didn't give one shit about what was going to happen to me, so don't expect me to be heartbroken over his death. Do you think he'd have given a shit if I'd died? No, of course he wouldn't. There's no getting over the fact that his death has come at a very convenient time for me. With a bit of luck, Davis will realise that he's done for now his protector's gone and fuck off. He's not up to the job and without Barron, he'll soon get found out.'

We mull it over whilst I serve up dinner and by the time we've finished eating, Barron's death seems like old news. A part of me feels ashamed that we're discussing him and Brett's career prospects in such a way while his family is probably in pieces.

But only a small part.

'You said there were rumours flying around?' I

chase the last forkful of lasagne around my plate and scoop it into my mouth.

Brett laughs. 'Yeah, talk about overactive imaginations. One rumour was that Barron was a secret drug addict and overdosed. Another was that he was with a prostitute and died *in flagrante*. The thought of it's enough to make you bring your breakfast up. I don't know who makes such stuff up, or why people believe half of it.'

'I suppose you'll find out the truth about what happened soon enough. Byersons won't want rumours like that getting around. It won't do their reputation any good.'

'Exactly. Anyway, enough about Barron, tell me what sort of day you've had.'

I place my knife and fork together on my plate and push it away and then pick up my wine glass and take a big glug of wine.

'Hey, what's wrong?' Brett looks concerned, and I reach out and place my hand on his.

'Hey, nothing to worry about. It's just that I saw something today that I wish I hadn't.'

Brett listens without interrupting while I tell him about Fen and Darius. I don't tell him I felt afraid of Darius when I was walking back to our house. I feel slightly ridiculous about it now and must have been slightly hysterical, because, although Darius is a vile bully, he's hardly going to attack me. But I can't deny that for a moment, I felt a genuine sense of danger coming from Darius after seeing how he'd treated Fen.

I'm no better than the gossips at Byersons; I have an overactive imagination and a worst-case scenario brain. It's a fault of mine and something that I can't seem to prevent myself from doing. I blew Wendy's letter out of all proportion and assumed that she was going to throw a hand grenade of the past at me and blow up my life. I need to stop this overthinking and try to be more measured and calmer in the future.

When I've finished speaking, Brett leans back in his chair, shaking his head.

'Christ, poor Fen.'

'I know. I feel so bad for her. What can we do to help her, Brett? There must be something we can do?'

He's quiet for a moment and then speaks. 'I don't think we should interfere.'

'What! We have to do something. He could really hurt her, or worse.'

Brett leans in across the table and studies my face.

'That's so sweet and typical of you, Nat, that you'd want to help, but realistically, you can't do anything.'

'I could report him to the police. I'm a witness. I saw what he did to her.'

'Oh Nat.' Brett shakes his head. 'What good do you think that would do? Do you think Fen would thank you for it?' Before I can answer, he continues. '*She* has to report it, Nat, not you. Fen has to be the one to go to the police. And she hasn't;

so she doesn't want to. All you can do is discretely let her know you know, and that you're there for her if she needs you. And she might not like that, either, so be prepared for her not being grateful or telling you that you've got it all wrong or to mind your own business.'

I sigh. On a sensible level, I know that he's right, but it doesn't seem okay to do nothing.

'Nat?'

I look up at him.

'Promise me you won't interfere. Just be there for her, yeah?'

'I promise,' I say. 'But I don't feel good about it. What if he really hurt her, Brett? What if he killed her? It would be my fault for not doing anything and I couldn't live with myself.'

'It wouldn't be your fault. It would be his. Besides, no one's going to kill anyone, Nat. I think you're getting a bit carried away.'

Brett is frowning and I know he's right; I'm catastrophizing again, doing my worst-case scenario thing.

'Sorry, I think I'm still in shock at what I saw. You know what I'm like for imagining the worst. It's just that I never imagined Darius was like that. No way did I take him for a vicious, wife-beating bully.'

Brett doesn't speak.

'He seemed such a gentleman and so in love with Fen, so protective and proud of her. Putting his arm around her and holding her hand and stuff. You must be as shocked as I am.'

There's silence for a second, and I wonder if Bret is still listening or his mind is elsewhere, thinking of work.

'No,' he says, quietly. 'I'm not shocked at all.'

CHAPTER
THIRTEEN

I'm on my way to meet Wendy.

After more than twenty years, I'm going to see my best friend again, the only best friend I've ever had. The girl, who just over a week ago, I was convinced was going to ruin my life.

I have the letter from Wendy to thank for the new me. If she hadn't contacted me, I'm not sure that I would ever have found the courage to tell Brett about my past. I would have carried on living my lie and each day that went by would have made it harder for me to tell him. Eventually, I think the strain would have become too much and our marriage wouldn't have survived.

Will I recognise her? Will she recognise me? We were eleven-years-old the last time we saw each other, we may have both changed beyond recognition. I have no photographs of myself as a child, so the picture in my head of what I looked like may not match the child I was. It's inevitable that Wendy will have changed, too. The skinny, dark-haired little girl with a heart-shaped face and freckles will have grown up and most likely look nothing like the girl I remember.

Wendy lives in the same town that we grew up in. I was beyond shocked when she told me this. I'd assumed that, like me, she would want to put as many miles between the past and the present as possible. After the fire we were both put in separate secure units far away from our hometown, but unlike me, maybe her mother visited her.

Did she go back and live with her mother?

She could well have done. Just because my father never bothered with me, doesn't mean that Wendy's mother did the same. She had a nan, too, who loved her, so she could have gone to live with her. Even so, I don't understand how she could want to return to a place that holds such awful memories.

There are a million questions I have for her, but I'm saving them until we meet. I didn't ask her anything by WhatsApp because it would have been an endless list. It'll be better to talk to her.

We're meeting in a town midway between where we both live. After an internet search, I found a pub online with excellent reviews, so I booked us a table for lunch; although I'm so nervous I'm not sure if I'll be able to eat anything.

It's a longer journey for Wendy, sixty miles to my fifty, but she was the one who suggested the town because it's straight down the motorway for her.

I try hard to concentrate on the road ahead but my mind insists on wandering. Memories from the past come back to me; things that I thought I'd forgotten. Not major, important things, but little things; silly games we used to play, slang words and sayings that we thought were so clever and sophisticated, corny jokes that we found hysterically funny. The pop songs we listened to on the radio and the dances we used to make up and practice repeatedly.

We were so young, and so innocent.

Until Wendy had her innocence taken away.

Even now, I still feel sick when I remember the day she told me. The memory of Wendy's near hysteria as she explained what Griff had done to her makes me anxious.

The satnav reminds me I need to pay attention and I listen carefully before indicating and taking the slip road off the motorway. I haven't been there before, so I have to concentrate on finding my way to the pub. I pay such close attention that I make no wrong turns and pull into the car park a whole thirty minutes too early. Parking in a bay furthest from the pub door, I kill the engine. I can see the pub entrance in my rear-view mirror, so I'll see if Wendy arrives. There are only three other cars in the car park, all empty of their drivers, so Wendy's not here yet. Although she could have arrived even earlier than me and already gone inside. One of those cars could be hers. I'll wait out here for a while before I go inside and check. I turn up the volume on the radio, unfasten my seat belt, and relax back into the seat before taking out my mobile phone and messaging Brett to let him know that I've arrived. He responds immediately with a thumbs up and a heart emoji. I smile and slip my mobile back into my handbag.

It's been a strange week; although Monday was only three days ago, the news of Barron's death and witnessing Darius abusing Fen, seems more like weeks ago. Brett's office is still in limbo, with no new manager in place, but Brett has a feeling that underneath the surface, arrangements and decisions are afoot. The finance director has been in constant contact with Brett, choosing him to speak to rather than any of the other fund managers. This is surely a good thing, and neither I nor Brett can stop ourselves from being optimistic. Davis hasn't shown his face at all and according to the telephone call Brett received on Tuesday, he's on a week's compassionate leave. The guys in the department chewed this over as no one takes compassionate leave unless it's a close relative. All they really want to know is if he's getting paid, and if he is, why? He's been working there for only a few months and the whiff of favouritism is in the air, because he's engaged to Barron's daughter.

The HR manager came down to the office and informed them of the official cause of Barron's death. Everyone pretended to be shocked even though they weren't. They already knew all about it from reading it in the online London News. Described as an accident in the home, Barron fell down the stairs resulting in immediate death from a broken neck. There's going to be an inquest, but that won't happen for several months. James from Brett's department phoned Davis—sucking up to him in case he comes back, Brett says—and got some more information from him. According to Davis, Barron got up in the early hours of the morning to get himself a glass of water, stumbled at the top of the stairs and plummeted down them head first. He lay at the bottom of the stairs all night until his wife got up the next morning and found him.

It would have been a quick death, according to London News.

So, not a heart attack as we predicted, just very bad luck.

As to Fen and Darius; I haven't seen Fen at all this week and I'm sure she's avoiding me. I messaged her on Tuesday morning and asked if she'd like to catch up with a coffee. She replied immediately that she had an awful cold and didn't feel great and also wouldn't want me to catch it. The same lie I told her when I wanted to avoid seeing her. She thanked me for the flowers and chocolates and added that she'd contact me as soon as she felt better.

I've heard nothing from her and it's now

Thursday.

I haven't messaged her since because I don't want to pester her, but I can't help worrying. Brett says I should leave her alone, and it's up to her to contact me. He's quite adamant that I shouldn't do anything. Their marriage is private and I'm to keep out of it. His reaction surprised me because he seemed to get on so well with Darius. I said this to him and he replied not to *keep on about them*, in an irritated way. It was nothing to do with us, he repeated, and why did I even want to get involved? I know that he's right. It's my overactive imagination again; my worst-case scenario brain thinking that Darius is going to murder Fen, or something ridiculous like that.

I tell myself that I'm letting my thoughts run away with themselves but I still don't feel good for Fen.

Twenty-five minutes to go.

Movement in the car mirror catches my attention and I twist around in my seat and watch as a red Fiesta drives into the car park. It reverses into a space on the opposite side of the car park and I turn around and peer into the mirror to get a look at the driver.

Is it Wendy?

Possibly. It's a woman with a mass of dark hair, but that's about all I can see. I open the car door, clamber out and stand and watch as she gets out of the car. She looks over at me and I take in her bright red coat and the fact that she's tiny, much shorter than my five-foot-seven. She's petite and doll-like. Dinky. She stares across at me for a second and then walks towards me. She's half-way across the car park when I know with absolute certainty.

It's Wendy.

* * *

The pub is quiet. Most of the other tables in the restaurant area are vacant, although there are a few people scattered along the bar. It's a weekday lunchtime so I suppose the place won't be heaving with customers.

Wendy and I are sitting at a table by the window that looks out over the car park; not the best of views, but it doesn't matter because we're not here for the scenery. Still, a part of me feels irritated that they've given us a crap table when the restaurant is practically empty. The tables with a view over the pretty garden are unoccupied and, unlike ours, don't have 'reserved' cards on them.

Wendy and I each have a menu in our hands, but we're not looking at the food choices, we're looking at each other.

'You've hardly changed a bit,' I say. 'I was afraid I wouldn't recognise you after all this time, but I knew straight away it was you.'

Wendy laughs, the same high-pitched tinkling laugh I remember and I'm transported to the past. I have a sudden, ridiculous wish to erase the last twenty years and start my life over again.

'I'm still a short-arse, if that's what you mean. Not like you. You've shot up, considering you weren't much taller than me when we were eleven.'

'I grew overnight when I turned twelve. I was like a baby giraffe.'

We laugh and I think how strange it is that after all this time, I feel so comfortable with her. We've slipped back into our friendship as if the last twenty years were a mere blink of the eye. She called me Holly when we greeted each other and I didn't correct her. It doesn't seem important. Like me, Wendy lived in care until she was eighteen; her nan died before she left the secure centre and although her mother visited her, she couldn't forgive her for setting fire to her home. Wendy stayed in care but unlike me, as soon as she could make her own choices, she returned to the town we were born and brought up in.

'You're married?' She's looking at my wedding ring. She doesn't wear one.

'I am. Three years. How about you?'

'No. Still waiting to meet *the one.*'

She's silent for a moment and then reaches across the table and takes hold of my hand.

'I was a mess,' she says. 'For a long time. Went from one man to another, could never settle. Always went for the bastards who treated me like shit. Was like that until I hit thirty. Finally got help when I tried to end it all with a bottle of vodka and a bottle of pills.'

I grip her hand.

'Is that why you've contacted me now?'

She nods. 'I tried to bury it, what happened. Him. Me. You. What we did. But it didn't work. Never works, does it? It's always there, underneath every smile, every lie, every almost moment of happiness. It's there, waiting to spoil it all; the big, dirty secret that never goes away.'

I want to cry, for Wendy, for me, but I don't. I wait.

'I got help, and it was tough, really tough. But I came through the other side. I'm not completely fixed and I don't think I ever will be, but I'm much better. I've stopped repeating the same mistakes. Mum and I see each other now and then. We always kept in touch, even when I was in care, but she couldn't forgive me for what I'd done.'

'I'm so glad you got help.'

'I should have told them, the police, what he did to me. He ruined both our lives, and I let him.'

'We were kids.' I shrug. 'We didn't know. We didn't think they'd believe us.'

'You'd think someone would have guessed, though, wouldn't you? I think they would nowadays. Anyway, better late than never. After I got help, I told Mum about Griff. What he did.'

'What did she say?'

'She didn't believe me. At first. At least, she pretended not to. I didn't even try to convince her because that wasn't what it was about; it didn't matter if she believed me, I just needed to say the words to her. I could see she was lying about not believing me and when she could see that I wasn't going to try to persuade her, she admitted that she believed me. She asked why I didn't tell her at the time. I told her I knew she wouldn't believe me. She couldn't really argue with that, could she? She preferred Griff to me. I could tell she wished I hadn't told her because I'd made it awkward for her.'

'Is that why you contacted me? Is it something the therapist advised you to do?'

'Sort of. I always wanted to find you, but I wasn't in a good place. I didn't want to mess your life up like I did before. You rescued me once and I couldn't let you do it again.'

I tell her then how I changed my name as soon as I was able and buried the truth about my past. How I've only just told Brett.

'You wouldn't believe how much I've missed you, Wendy, how much I've thought about you over the years.'

She smiles and I can tell she's pleased.

'I've missed you too, so much. It must have been so hard for you, living a lie for so long, Natalie. Natalie. I like it, the name suits you.'

'It was hard for both of us. We should have told the truth then, when we got caught. We should have trusted them to believe us.'

'Things were different then. The way our lives were, we thought no one would believe anything we said. But that's in the past now; all that matters is that we're okay now, we're over it and we've moved on.'

The waitress appears and we quickly choose a meal from the menu, both opting for the obvious choice of steak and chips. When the waitress has gone, I pick up my glass.

'A toast,' I say, holding my glass of orange juice aloft. 'To us.'

Wendy picks up her glass, and we chink them together and take a sip.

'We'll keep in touch after today, won't we?' I ask.

'Of course.' Wendy puts her glass down. 'But I have something that I need to say to you. It's something I never got the chance to say all those years ago.'

I look at her with a questioning look, wondering what she's talking about.

'Thank you for what you did for me.'

I shake my head. 'You don't need to thank me, Wendy, you really don't.'

'I do.' She leans across the table. 'You sacrificed your life when you saved me. Thank you for doing what I didn't have the guts to do myself.'

CHAPTER FOURTEEN

Fen messaged me this morning and invited me over for coffee. It's nearly two weeks since she said she had a terrible cold and cancelled on me and now, out of the blue, she's contacted me.

What could I say? Well, yes, of course, because what else is there to say? I messaged her last week, because I hadn't heard from her for over a week and she replied that her cold had turned into the flu. She thanked me for my offer to help but said she was fine as Darius was looking after her. The message didn't sound like Fen at all.

Did Darius write it?

It was my overactive imagination again, Brett said, when I voiced my concern to him. His attitude is that they're just neighbours and we should keep our distance. In his words, *he's a wife-*

beater, so why do we want them as friends?

I know that he's right, and not seeing either of them has made it easier for me to not get hung up with guilt for not doing anything about what I saw. Or thought I saw; maybe my imagination ran away with me again; maybe it wasn't half as bad as I think it was.

What can I do, anyway?

I don't want to see Fen. I no longer yearn to make her my friend. Her problems will become mine if she confides in me and quite honestly, I don't want that.

Does that make me shallow and heartless? Yes, it probably does; but I'm not going to beat myself up about it. As Brett says, we hardly know them and there's no reason for us to involve ourselves in their marriage. Neither of them would thank us for sticking our noses in because what goes on behind their closed doors is none of our business. If Fen asked me for help, that would be different, but she hasn't, and I don't think she will.

I've changed. There's no denying it. Telling Brett the truth about my past has freed me from the constant fear of being found out. I'm no longer terrified that my past will come out and ruin my life. I still have the guilt of Griff's death, but I justify that with what he did to Wendy. It's only now that she's coming to terms with and getting over what he did to her, after all those years. At least he never got to abuse any other girls. Men like him don't stop, they just find new victims.

Pieces of shit like that don't deserve to live, according to Brett.

He's right, who knows how many other lives he would have ruined had he lived.

Now that Wendy is back in your life, you're not interested in Fen anymore, the honest part of me accuses.

Sort of true. Wendy and I were the best of friends when we were children, but realistically, we're never going to have that closeness again. It was different then. Two kids with rotten home lives clinging together because we had nothing else. We were everything to each other but we're grown up now. It's not the same. We'll always be friends, good friends, but we're never going to have the closeness that we once had. I'm married and Brett is always going to come first. Wendy and I will keep in touch and meet up now and again, but she won't be a major part of my life, nor I hers. There's the physical distance, for a start, and we're both very different people to the children we once were. Wendy is much stronger now. She doesn't need me to look after her. Now that Brett knows about my past, I don't have the need or desire to unburden myself to anyone else.

Two-thirty-five.

I'll have to go over and have coffee with Fen. She didn't specify a time, but I know she'll be expecting me about now. If I put it off any longer, it'll look as if I don't want to see her.

I don't.

I slip my coat on and open the front door. Despite being mid-afternoon, the sky is a dark, threatening grey. The wind cuts into me as I step outside and take the short walk across the street and up the driveway to their house. I hadn't bothering doing up my coat so I wrap it around me, holding it closed with my arms. The lounge lights are shining through their bay window blinds, giving the house a cosy and inviting look.

I don't want to go in.

Forcing myself to march straight up the porch steps, I ring the bell before I can change my mind, turn around and go home. I fix a smile on my face that is as fake as I feel for even being here. I'll stay for an hour-and-a-half and then make my excuses and leave.

Tell her you're ill, was Brett's response when I messaged him this morning. *I can't,* I messaged back, *she'll know I'm lying.* He sent a laughing face emoji with *that's the whole point, because she'll take the hint and leave you alone.*

I couldn't bring myself to do it; Fen's a nice person and it's cruel.

Through the frosted glass in the door, I see the outline of a figure coming down the hallway towards me. The figure draws closer and as the door is opened, my fears are confirmed.

It's Darius.

'Natalie! How lovely to see you! Come in, come in.' He steps to one side and waits for me to go in.

'I thought I'd join you and Fen for coffee as I'm

working from home today. You don't mind, do you?' He flashes his megawatt smile at me as he closes the front door.

'Of course not,' I lie. 'It'll be great to catch up.'

'Just what I said to Fen.' He ushers me down the hallway and into the lounge, where Fen is waiting.

I wish I'd sent that message now, cruel or not.

* * *

'No.'

'But...'

'No, Nat, there's no way I'm sitting in their house playing happy families with them. No. Make an excuse. Lie. Say we're already doing something. God knows we've got enough real friends that we never get to see. If it makes you feel better, we could actually go out with our friends next Saturday and then you won't be lying. Charlie and Jenna are always asking us to go up west with them. I'll give Charlie a call.'

'It'll look so obvious.'

'I don't care. They're just neighbours, Nat. We don't have to explain ourselves to them.'

I knew Brett wouldn't be keen, but I never realised how set he was on distancing us from them. I thought he liked Darius, and I can't believe that he's turned against him so quickly, despite what I told him I saw.

'You should have messaged her like I said and then we wouldn't be in this position.' He undoes his tie from around his neck, rips it off and tosses it onto the sofa next to the jacket that's already lying there. I watch the back of him as he stands at the sideboard, pouring himself a drink. The set of his shoulders and the way he crashes the bottle around tells me that there's no talking to him now.

So much for choosing the right moment.

Today the department learned that they have a new manager. It's someone Brett knows, but more importantly, he's already friendly with him. As if that wasn't enough amazing news, he's also been officially told that he's getting his bonus this year.

Great news that just a few weeks ago seemed impossible.

He should be ecstatic, but although he said he was pleased, his behaviour suggests otherwise.

'What's wrong, Brett?'

'What do you mean, what's wrong?'

'I thought you'd be over the moon about your bonus and Barron's replacement, but you don't seem that happy.'

'Fuck's sake, Nat, give me a break.' He tosses a mouthful of whisky down his throat. 'I've just been through the most stressful few months of my life. An axe has been hanging over my head, ready to fall at any fucking moment.'

'I know and I'm sorry, but it's all going to be okay now. Better than okay. We couldn't have asked for anything more.'

He doesn't answer, and I wonder if he's even listening to me.

Why the hell did I go to Fen's? If I'd stayed away, we wouldn't be talking about it now and heading for a row over a stupid dinner invitation. The visit for coffee was an excruciating hour-and-a-half of my life that I'll never get back. Fen looked ill and kept coughing, so maybe she wasn't lying about having the flu. Her skin was so pale it looked translucent and she seemed even thinner than normal. She hardly spoke whilst Darius kept up a constant monologue of jokey anecdotes about his business. It was excruciating. The strain of laughing in the right places whilst not really listening to what he was saying was almost more than I could bear.

What was I supposed to say when they asked us to dinner again? I protested it was their turn to come to us, hoping that I could put them off, but Fen wouldn't hear of it. One of the few times she spoke, she was insistent that we go to them. She needed something to do and to plan for after being bed bound for two weeks, she said.

What was I supposed to say?

I tried vague excuses about Brett being busy and having to check with him, and Darius laughed uproariously. If he didn't know me better, he said, he'd think I was trying to get out of it. He looked right at me when he said it, the trademark grin gone for a moment, as if he knew I was lying.

Maybe he did; maybe I'm not such a good liar as I think.

Backed into a corner, I had to accept their offer.

I put them off for this weekend, lying that we were going out with other friends, but agreed that next Saturday we'd go to theirs for dinner. I couldn't see any way of refusing.

Remote control in hand, Brett flops onto the sofa and turns on the TV.

'I'll start dinner.' Maybe if I leave him alone for a while, his mood will improve.

'I'm not hungry.'

'You might be by the time I've cooked it.'

'I'm not. Don't waste your time cooking me anything.'

I stare at him but he refuses to look at me, instead concentrating on the TV screen.

'You should eat something.'

'This is all I need.' He holds the whisky tumbler up in one hand whilst staring at the screen, turning up the volume on the remote control in the other. The volume is so loud that even if I spoke, he wouldn't hear me. I stare at him for a moment and then turn and head towards the kitchen.

Fuck off Brett.

* * *

When we got up this morning, Brett decided that today was the perfect day to clean his golf clubs.

We ate breakfast in silence and after announcing what he intended to do; he went out to the garage and I haven't seen him since. I'm guessing he's still angry about the dinner invitation with Fen and Darius, but the cold shoulder he's giving me seems way out of proportion to the situation.

Fuming, I remove the breakfast dishes and throw them into the dishwasher, feeling oddly pleased when I snap a plate in half. *That'll teach him*, I mutter, as I hurl the pieces into the bin. Exactly how it's going to teach him, I don't know.

The weekend stretches ahead; a vision of Brett in a cold, monosyllabic mood for the next two days. I feel furious at him for being so childish. Determined not to wait around the house until his mood improves or alternatively, I hit him, I run upstairs and get changed into my running gear.

The garage door is half-open as I run down the driveway, but I don't bother stopping to go in and speak to him; why give him the chance to ignore me and put me in an even worse mood?

No. Sod him.

Jogging down the street, I cross the road and break into a run and head towards the park. Racing past the regular Saturday morning dog-walkers and joggers, I pound along towards the lake. I've brought some money with me and intend treating myself to a pastry and a latte at the vegan coffee shop on the other side of the park. The café is ridiculously over-priced and snobbish, but it beats hanging around the house with a sulking husband. First lap completed, I exit the park from the rear entrance and slow down to a walk as I emerge onto the street.

When I reach the café, I sit at a table by the window so I can watch the Saturday shoppers go by. The pastry is stale and the latte quite tasteless, but I finish them both because leaving the pastry on the plate would look insulting. I'm the only customer in this tiny café, and if this is the regular fare, I can see why. It's awful. I'm embarrassed for the owner when I leave the café because I was the only person sitting in there on a busy high street. I wonder if I'll be their only customer all day?

I head back along the street and into the park and am just about to speed up, when I see them.

Brett and Darius.

I slow to a stop and look over at them. There's no mistaking Darius. He stands out a mile due to the sheer size of him. I look at Brett to make sure that it is him and not someone who looks like him. It most definitely is him. I'm stunned to see them together after the way Brett spoke. They're standing by the edge of the lake, looking out over the water, and neither one of them has seen me. Hands thrust into his pockets, Brett is staring at the water whilst Darius talks. I jog quickly back to the outside of the park and stand behind the tall brick pillars on either side of the gates, out of sight.

For some reason, I feel as if I'm intruding, but I don't know why. I don't want them to see me. They're deep in conversation and I wonder why they're in the park and not in our street. After several minutes, they begin to walk slowly along by the lake. I hurriedly step back, but I've no need to worry because they haven't seen me as they're not looking in my direction. I debate whether to continue my run through the park. They'd be unlikely to see me unless I was really unlucky and one of them turned around. I decide not to risk it, because I want to be the one surprising Brett, not the other way around. I could, and probably should, say hello and stop sneaking around, but I'm not going to. Brett has royally pissed me off and I'm going to make him squirm when I tell him I've seen him talking with Darius as if they're the best of friends.

It'll take a lot longer to get home by running through the streets, but I console myself with the fact that it'll be excellent exercise. As I run, I'm already rehearsing what I'm going to say to Brett when he tells me he's seen Darius, and that dinner is back on. I wonder how long it will take him. I'm stunned that after everything Brett's had to say about Darius and Fen, he now goes for a walk in the park with him.

The hypocrite.

He's got some grovelling to do.

CHAPTER FIFTEEN

I'm sweating and my legs are aching by the time I get back to the house. As I walk up the driveway, I see the garage door is ajar and I duck my head to see if Brett is in there.

He is; feet planted apart, he's standing in front of his golf bag and I guess he's still cleaning them. Or pretending to. He doesn't fool me. They weren't even dirty to start with. I continue to the front door without stopping to call out to him. He'll have heard my feet crunching up the driveway, so must know I'm back. I unlock the front door and go in and in the few minutes it takes me, Brett makes no move to come out of the garage and talk to me. Surely now that he and Darius are back to being friends, he can't still be pissed off at me about the dinner date.

I'll play it cool and see how long it takes him

to tell me that dinner next Saturday is now most definitely *on*. He isn't aware that I already know and may well pretend to have changed his mind so he can behave as if he's doing me a massive favour.

We'll see about that, mister, you've been rumbled.

I go upstairs and shower and wash my hair and by the time I've dressed and dried my hair, it's close to one o'clock. After I check the lounge, I go out into the kitchen. There's still no sign of him. How long does it take to pretend to clean a set of golf clubs?

As if he can hear my thoughts, the internal door from the garage opens, and he comes into the kitchen.

'Hi. Have you come in for some lunch?'

He stops mid-stride and stares at me without emotion.

'Lunch?' I prompt. 'It's nearly one o'clock.'

'I'm not hungry.'

He's still being off with me. How fucking dare he.

'What have you been up to all morning?' I ask, suddenly exhausted with him taking his bad mood out on me.

He blinks, as if I've asked him an extremely difficult question, before replying.

'Cleaning my golf clubs.'

'Wow, they must have been disgustingly dirty.' I sound as if I'm being sarcastic. I am being sarcastic.

He shrugs but doesn't answer and walks across the kitchen towards the hallway.

'Don't you want to know what I've been doing all morning?'

'You've been in here,' he calls over his shoulder.

'No, I haven't, actually.' I follow him out into the hallway. 'I've been out for a run and I'm surprised you never noticed me come back, as you had the garage door open.'

He turns in the lounge doorway and looks at me without interest.

'I went for a run.' I say. 'In the park.'

And there it is, the merest flinch when I mentioned the park.

'You didn't say you were going out.' He walks into the lounge, no longer looking at me, throwing the words over his shoulder.

'Nor did you,' I counter.

He stops and turns. 'Cleaning my golf clubs in the garage isn't going out.'

I stare at him. This is so typical of Brett. He won't want to admit that going to dinner at Fen and Darius's is back on, because he made such a bloody fuss about it in the first place.

'You haven't been out?'

'No.'

'You didn't go to the park?'

'No, I've been in the garage. *Cleaning my golf clubs,*' he says slowly, enunciating each word, as if I'm having trouble understanding him. 'If that's the inquisition over, I thought I'd put the telly on and watch football, if that's all right with you.' He continues into the lounge and I glare at his back as he goes, struggling to understand why he's being so off with me. I stomp after him and stand in front of him as he settles himself in the armchair and turns the TV on, blocking his view of the TV screen.

'You never went to the park?' I demand.

'No. I did not go to the park. For fuck's sake, Nat, give it a rest, will you?'

'I saw you there.' There's that flicker in his eyes again. Guilt that I've found him out.

'No. You didn't. I wasn't at the park and I don't know why you're obsessed with the fucking place. Now can you get out of the way because you're blocking the telly.'

'I saw you. Talking to Darius by the lake. You might as well admit it, because I know what I saw. You were chatting together, deep in conversation, so you can stop being shitty with me. I know you're best chums with him again so you can stop behaving as if I've done something wrong just because I accepted a dinner invitation from them.'

By the time I finish, I'm angry and almost shouting. Seething, I fold my arms and stare down at Brett and wait for him to admit he was wrong.

'You need to get your eyes tested,' he states. 'I haven't seen Darius. Why would I want to see him?'

'I saw you, Brett.'

'No,' he says, standing up and throwing the

remote control onto the armchair. 'You didn't. You saw someone who looked like me, or you imagined it or dreamed it. Who knows? I don't know who you saw, but you never saw me.'

He storms across the room and out into the hallway and I'm still standing there, mouth open in shock, when I hear the front door slam.

I saw him; I know I did.

He's lying.

But why?

* * *

I stare at the oven door as if it will speak to me and tell me what to do. Brett came home at five o'clock, just walked in as if he'd left the house five minutes earlier.

He didn't say where he'd been, and I didn't ask.

He headed straight to the lounge, and I waited for ten minutes before joining him. Slumped in the armchair with the TV on full blast, he was pretending to watch it. I knew he wasn't really watching because the programme was about fixing up old houses and there's no way he would watch anything DIY. He hates that sort of programme.

I asked him if he was okay and he said he was fine. I attempted to make conversation, but he responded with monosyllabic answers and avoided eye contact. He couldn't even look at me. I opened my mouth to ask him what was wrong, but closed it again without speaking. He won't talk to me when he's in a mood like that, so it was pointless to try. And the TV volume was so loud I had to practically shout to make myself heard. Right now, I'm so pissed off because it feels as if he's been behaving this way for weeks, and I suppose he has, on and off. He was in a stinking mood when he thought he was going to lose his job but then got over it, so I know it'll pass, but at this moment, that doesn't help. It seems almost laughable when I remember his promise to talk to me and not to cut me out again.

Something's wrong, that much I know, but that doesn't stop me from wanting to slap him for behaving like a spoilt brat. I feel like shaking him.

But I'm also worried about him.

I cannot, for the life of me, understand why he's lying about something as trivial as talking to Darius. After he'd stormed out this afternoon, I paced around the lounge and tried to make sense of it. I saw them together; there is no doubt about that in my mind, so why is Brett lying? They must have arranged to meet, because it wouldn't cross Brett's mind to go for a walk around the park, so they couldn't have met by chance. As far as I'm aware, he's never been to the park once since we moved here.

I thought about going to see Darius while Brett was out. I went as far as putting on my coat and actually had my hand on the front door handle, ready to open it, before I came to my senses. What stopped me from walking across that road and demanding Darius tell me what was going on was that he was unlikely to tell me anything. If Brett wouldn't tell me himself, Darius is unlikely to break his confidence.

Also, how embarrassing would it be to ask a neighbour what they'd been talking about because my husband won't tell me?

Mortifying.

Whilst Brett was gone, I veered between anger at him for freezing me out again, and fear that something terrible is going on and he can't bring himself to tell me. Brett is insistent that Darius isn't a friend, just a neighbour, so what were they talking about?

None of it makes sense.

When he came home, hours later, my anger was gone, and I just felt relieved that he was home. My overactive imagination was roaming wild by then, and the next step would have been ringing around all the hospitals to see if he'd had an accident. I bit my tongue and instead of firing questions at him, which is what I wanted to do, I went into the kitchen to prepare dinner.

I couldn't quite leave it, though.

Because here I am, chopping vegetables and now and then, I sneak along the hallway and peer round the lounge doorway to see what he's doing. Each time he hasn't moved from the armchair and is staring at the TV or looking at his phone. I then come back into the kitchen and resume chopping.

Once I've prepped dinner and laid the table, I pace around while I try to figure out what the hell is going on.

Talk to me, Brett. Just tell me.

I open a bottle of red wine and place two glasses on the table. Maybe a drink will relax him, make him open up. Mediterranean chicken, dauphinoise potatoes and green beans; one of his, and my, favourite meals. I turn the oven off and place the dishes on the table between us. There, it looks and smells delicious. I saunter into the lounge as if I don't have a care in the world and announce that dinner is ready. Brett raises his head from his phone and looks at me blankly.

'Dinner's ready,' I repeat.

For a moment, I think he's going to say he's not hungry, but he doesn't. He slides his phone into his jeans pocket and stands up. Without speaking, he walks past me and down the hallway towards the kitchen. I bite down the anger that threatens to explode out of me and follow him. He's already sitting at the table when I get there and I slide into the seat opposite him. He spoons food onto his plate and I wait until he's finished before doing the same.

I soon realise that I've wasted my time cooking. Clearly, none of the food is going to get eaten by either of us. The chicken tastes like cardboard in my mouth and Brett is pushing everything around on his plate, but eating very little of it. He's placed his phone face down next to his plate so that I can't see the screen. It beeps several times with incoming text messages.

'You're popular tonight,' I say, chewing a lump of potato that refuses to go down.

''What?'

'Your phone.' I nod at it. 'Someone's sending you a lot of texts.'

He doesn't answer, but places his knife and fork together on the plate and pushes it away.

'I'm not hungry. Sorry.' He doesn't sound sorry. 'Think I must have some sort of bug.'

His phone beeps again, and he picks it up, glances at the screen before putting it down again.

'Not going to reply?'

'No.'

'Brett, what's wrong? Please tell me. You promised you wouldn't shut me out again and here we are; you won't speak to me.'

'Nothing's wrong. All I want is a bit of peace and quiet. I don't feel like talking and anyway, we don't have to talk everything to death.'

'I know it was you in the park,' I mutter. 'So why are you lying about something so stupid?'

His phone beeps again, and I look pointedly at it.

Brett suddenly stands up.

'For fuck's sake, give it a rest. I wasn't in the park and there's nothing wrong. I just want you to leave me alone. That's not a lot to ask, is it? And don't accuse me of lying when you lied to me from the day you met me. And you kept on lying for years; so don't you dare take the fucking moral high ground with me.'

My anger is slipping, and I want to cry. Swallowing it down, knowing that crying now will make everything worse, I try to keep my voice level and not let him see how upset I am.

'I thought you were okay about my past. We talked about it and you said you understood and that we were alright, that we'd come through it.'

He sighs. 'It is. It's alright. Don't worry. Forget I said it, I'm sorry. I just need some space to think. Not everything's about you and I can't think if you keep nagging me and pestering me to talk to you.'

'Okay. Don't bother talking to me. I'm only your wife, after all.'

He doesn't answer and when his phone beeps again; he picks it up and glances at it before putting it down. Anger floods through me that he'd rather look at his phone than speak to me.

'Maybe I should ask Darius what's going on because you don't seem to have any trouble talking to him, do you?'

Brett glares at me and I wait for him to erupt; this is it. This is where we have a huge row and I get to find out what's going on.

'Don't you dare.' His voice is a low growl, and he has a look on his face that I've never seen before.

'Why not? You won't tell me anything.'

He stands up, pushing the chair back roughly. It teeters for an instant before falling to the floor with a crash. His eyes are blazing and his mouth is set in a grim line. Without warning, he lunges across the table and grips the tops of my arms. I gasp as his fingers bite into the flesh before he lets go. Snatching his phone from the table, he leans over me, pushing his face close to mine.

'If you talk to him, Nat,' he hisses. 'We're done.'

* * *

I open my eyes and stare into the darkness. Somehow, I fell asleep last night. It seems incredible that I could sleep after what Brett said to me. His words have been whirling around in my head since dinner, and I've been trying to make sense of them ever since.

Talk to him and we're done.

There's something badly wrong, and I've missed whatever it is. I thought we were okay after I told him about my past. I thought that our marriage was going to be better.

It's not.

Perhaps he was talking to Darius about me, telling him how I've lied to him since the day we met. Who could blame him? Maybe he's not okay with it, maybe he'll never be okay with it.

I feel sick.

And betrayed, although I have no right to after what I did to him.

Or maybe it's nothing to do with me, maybe, as Brett says, not everything is about me.

Is he having an affair?

A few months ago, I would have said it was

impossible, but now, I'm not so sure.

Anything is possible.

Brett has always told me he hates cheats; from the day we first met, he impressed upon me that the thing that would split us up for sure would be if one of us cheated. He'd never cheated on any of his previous girlfriends because he could never see the point. If a relationship is that bad, end it. I've always trusted him implicitly, but now I can't help doubting him. He's behaving so strangely. The constant text messages, the lying about seeing Darius, and now the threat that we're over if I dare to even approach him.

It could be another woman. What else would make him behave like this? He has plenty of opportunity; he's good-looking and successful and women are always eyeing him up when we're out together. Some of his friends' wives can't stop themselves from checking him out when they think no one's looking when we're on a night out with them. He works in a large company with lots of women employees; he plays squash and goes to the gym, he often works late. There are a hundred ways he could have met someone.

My insecurities about not being good enough for him are resurfacing fast; I never could believe that he could love someone like me.

Closing my eyes, I try to drift off to sleep because if I stay on this train of thought; I'll be up all night. I breathe in slowly through my mouth and out through my nose to relax myself.

Which is when I realise that aside from my breathing, the bedroom is silent.

Brett isn't in bed next to me.

He was here before I fell asleep. I came to bed at ten o'clock last night because I couldn't stand the frosty atmosphere in the lounge. Neither of us spoke all evening, and we spent the evening staring at the TV. I was still wide awake when Brett came to bed hours later, although I pretended to be asleep. I pick up my phone from the bedside table to see that it's three-thirty-five.

Where is he?

I get out of bed and go out onto the landing. The house is silent and as I peer down the stairs, I see a glow of light in the hallway. I pad down the stairs in my bare feet and as I get to the bottom step, I see a narrow strip of light showing from underneath the closed door of the lounge. I walk across the hallway and open the door to see Brett standing in front of the sideboard with his back to me, tumbler of whisky in hand.

'Brett?'

Silence. I may as well go back to bed; he won't speak to me. He turns around and the light from the table lamp shines on him; his face is pale and he looks gaunt, not himself at all. It suddenly hits me that he could be ill and can't bring himself to tell me. I walk over to him and put my arms around him, expecting him to push me away, but he doesn't. He wraps his arms around me and grips me so tightly that I can scarcely breathe. I feel the edge of the glass tumbler he's holding cutting into my back.

'Oh, Nat,' he murmurs.

'It's alright.' I rub his back. 'It's alright.'

'No, it's not.' He takes a deep, shuddering breath. 'It's not alright, and it's all my fault.'

'What's your fault?' I pull away from him so I can look at his face.

'Everything.' He pauses for a moment. 'I've done something so stupid, Nat, and there's no way out.'

CHAPTER SIXTEEN

There's guilt written all over his face. I wait for him to tell me what I've feared—that he's having an affair.

Am I going to forgive him?

I don't know.

'You'd better sit down.' Releasing his hold of me, he flops down into the armchair. He could have sat on the sofa next to me, but he chose not to. He's keeping his distance. I perch on the edge of the sofa and brace myself, waiting for him to utter the words that will destroy our marriage.

He takes a mouthful of whisky and I have an impulse to snatch the tumbler from his hand and hurl it against the wall. I clench my fists, my fingernails cutting into my palms. Get it over with, Brett, just rip the plaster off and say it.

'It's my fault that Barron is dead.'

'What?' I stare at him unable to comprehend what he's talking about.

'It's my fault. I killed him.'

The relief that he's not having an affair is replaced by bewilderment. I was not expecting this. What on earth is he talking about?

'Barron?' I repeat. 'You're not making any sense. How can you have possibly killed him when he fell down the stairs? It was an accident, Brett. He fell down the stairs in the middle of the night. You didn't kill him.'

'No, no, you don't understand.' He looks as if he's going to cry and I jump up from the sofa and go to him. I sit on his lap and wrap my arms around him and pull him close.

'I feel so guilty. If it wasn't for me, he'd still be alive. I hated him and now he's dead because of me.'

'Brett, listen, just because you wished him dead doesn't make it your fault. You didn't make it happen. It was an accident.'

He pushes me away and drags his hand across his face and rubs his eyes.

'It wasn't an accident. He made it *look* like an accident but it was murder. And I'm the one responsible.'

All thoughts of Brett having an affair, my anger and annoyance at him, have vanished.

'How was this murder made to look like an accident? Tell me, because you were here in bed with me when it happened. It's guilt that's making you feel this way. GUILT. Believe me, I know what I'm talking about because I've carried guilt around with me since I was eleven-years-old. You're not thinking straight, Brett. I think you've been working too hard and got confused.'

'No, you don't understand. It's my fault. I don't know the details. I don't *want* to know the details, but I know Barron was murdered. It's what he does.'

'It's what who does? Who are you talking about?'

'Darius.' He whispers his name as if he might hear us.

'Darius?'

'Yes. It's his job. It's what he does. He kills people.'

I stare at him in disbelief. Darius? Our neighbour across the road?

'He's got an export company, Brett. He's a businessman, not a hitman.'

'Oh, God.' Brett rakes his fingers across his head, clenching a fistful of hair. 'Why did we ever have to meet him? Why did he have to move into this fucking street? Why?'

'Brett, calm down, because seriously, why would Darius do that? Kill Barron? He didn't even know him.' I'm humouring him; trying to calm him down. Does he honestly believe that we live across the road from a killer? Half of me wants to laugh hysterically. The other half of me wants to cry at the state that Brett is in. It's guilt that's making him feel like this.

'Money. Nat, he makes money, so much money. He gets rid of obstacles, that's what he calls them. He gets rid of obstacles for people who pay him.'

'What, like a hitman?' I cannot keep the disbelief from my voice.

'I suppose you could call him that. He prefers to call himself an *enabler*. He makes it look like an accident, if he can, so that the police don't investigate too thoroughly.'

'Okay, tell me exactly what's happened and we can figure a way out of this.' He seems unaware that I'm humouring him, and even as I listen, I wonder what the hell I'm going to do. I stare at my husband sitting in front of me and it's obvious that he's having some sort of breakdown. He's ill. The last few months of stress at work have been too much for him. While I've been selfishly wrapped up in reflections about my own life, Brett has been quietly falling apart and I haven't even noticed. I feel disgust at my self-centredness but I push it away; wallowing in regret won't help Brett now.

He needs help.

'It was that night we went for dinner at theirs, when I got pissed. Darius was friendly and easy to talk to. He was interested in what I was saying and I guess I got carried away and said more than I should. I was ranting on about work, saying what a bastard Barron was, and he was sympathetic and seemed to understand how I was feeling. I said how much better the place would be without

Barron, but I never wanted him dead. No way did I ask him to kill him. I wouldn't do that. I wouldn't. I was drunk and ranting, that's all.'

'Is that when he told you he was a hitman or an enabler, or whatever he calls himself?'

'I can't remember. Maybe. I was so wasted I don't know.'

'You think you might have said you wanted Barron dead?' We're talking as if this is actually real but I have to know how bad it is; how bad Brett is.

'No, I wouldn't have done that. I hated him, but I didn't want him dead. No way would I have said that. I've never said it to you, have I? That I wished he was dead, so why would I say it to him? Darius says I did, though. Told me he wouldn't have done it if I hadn't asked him to. He says we had an agreement and now I have to pay.'

'How much does he want?'

'He's dangerous,' he says, not answering my question. 'Once I pay, he'll have me for life, Nat. We'll never be free of him.'

'You don't have to pay him, because how can he prove he murdered Barron? He can't, because Barron's death was an accident. He's lying to you, conning you into believing that he killed Barron. His death was accidental, and he's trying to rip you off.'

Brett shakes his head, muttering *you don't understand.*

The two of them meeting in the park yesterday,

Darius talking while Brett listened. Burning hot anger builds in me. Whilst I was engrossed in my own problems, Darius saw Brett was vulnerable and having some sort of breakdown and he exploited it. Brett isn't at all gullible normally, but the last few months have clearly taken their toll.

'He's trying to con you because Barron's death was an unfortunate accident. He fell down the stairs in the middle of the night and no one can fake that. The police aren't even investigating it because they know it was an accident.'

He gets up and pours himself another whisky before replying.

'No, he killed him, or had him killed. It doesn't matter how he did it. He's clever, that's why no one has ever caught him. You don't know what he's capable of. He's killed others, lots of them, he told me.'

'Just because he told you, it doesn't make it true. Think about it Brett; he's taking you for a fool.'

I look up at Brett; I mean, really look at him. He's lost weight over the last few months and I wonder how I haven't noticed.

You were too absorbed in yourself.

I was; and I'll have to live with that. Brett is ill; his skin is pale and there are dark shadows underneath his eyes. I think back over the past months and realise that he must have been struggling for a while. The stress at work has worn him down and that, coupled with the huge mortgage we've taken on, has been too much for him. I see now that he's changed in other ways, too. We've hardly seen our friends recently, whereas we used to have a hectic social life. The only social event we've been to in the last few months is to Fen and Darius's house for dinner. This is unlike Brett; he's sociable and a week never went by when we weren't going out or meeting up with friends. I knew we hadn't been out for a while but because it suited me—they're Brett's friends and not mine —I never asked myself, or Brett, why, because I was quite happy not seeing them. My life was easier when I didn't have to try with people who made me feel inferior and somehow lacking. Darius is nothing but a conman with the gift of the gab and Brett has fallen for it hook, line and sinker. As well as being a wife-beater he's a crook who befriends and manipulates people in order to exploit them.

'I'm not a fool.' Brett stops pacing and stands in front of me. 'He's dangerous. The reason I went to the park yesterday was because I didn't want him coming here. I don't want him in our house. I know it all sounds ridiculous, but it's true. I have proof. Darius sent me messages after Barron died, warning me what would happen if I didn't settle with him. I ignored them; I read them but never replied. He sent so many that in the end I blocked his number. I thought, no, hoped, that would stop him. I couldn't stand reading them because it was stressing me out.'

'So what happened?'

'I got a message from an unknown number.

I knew it was him using another phone. The message said that there was no point in deleting his number because he would just use another phone. Or pay me a visit in person. I knew it was a threat. And then another message came through straight afterwards. A woman's name.'

'What woman?'

'I don't know. Nobody I knew. The name meant nothing to me.' He walks over to the chair, picks up his mobile and comes and sits down on the sofa next to me. He scrolls through the messages and then hands the mobile to me.

'Look.'

Helen Wenham.

'See?' He jumps up from the sofa, unable to sit still.

'No, I don't see.'

'Scroll down to the next message.'

I flick my finger down the screen.

'It's a link?'

'Click on it.'

I tap the link and wait for it to load. It's a newspaper report about a woman found battered to death in her flat in London. I read the whole thing and then look up at Brett.

'The woman's name is Helen Wenham,' I say. 'The name he sent you.'

'Now do you see?'

'No, I don't. He's playing games with you; trying to make out he's some sort of hitman when he's just a conman. Just because he sent you an article about a murder doesn't mean that *he* murdered her. He's trying to frighten you.' I can't believe he's being so gullible.

'Fuck's sake, Nat!' Brett shouts. 'Look at the date. LOOK AT THE DATE.'

He snatches the mobile from my hands and holds the screen up in front of my eyes.

'LOOK,' he shouts. 'He sent me the woman's name *before* she was murdered.'

I take the phone from him and study the screen. I check the date of the first message, then the date he sent the link. Clicking on the article, I reread it. The date of the article is three days after Darius sent the message with the woman's name.

And one day after Helen Wenham was beaten to death.

'Now, do you believe me?'

'It must be a trick,' I say, not wanting to believe it. 'He's tricked you somehow.'

'How? Tell me how, because I can't think of any way he could know she was going to die two days before she was battered to death unless he murdered her. If you can think of a way, then tell me. Please.'

As hard as I try, I can't think of a way he could have known. He killed her; he must have killed her, because otherwise how could he know she was going to die?

I feel sick.

'What are we going to do?' I ask, my voice a whisper.

Brett sits down and puts his arm around me.

'I told him I'd give him what he wants. I don't want anyone else to die because of me. He's shown me what he's capable of.'

I think about it.

'Don't pay him; we can go to the police. You've done nothing wrong and there's no proof you had anything to do with anyone's death, the woman's or Barron's. Darius is the one who's incriminated himself. We can tell the police everything, show them the messages. It's nothing to do with you. It's not your fault he's a madman.'

'Police?' Brett looks alarmed. 'Christ, no, we can't go to the police. I've told you what he's capable of. You've seen what he's done.'

'The police will protect us. They'll arrest him and then we'll be safe. He won't be able to hurt us from a prison cell.'

'You think they'll be able to prove anything? The only evidence is a few messages on my phone and how will they prove he sent them? It'll be my word against his. They probably won't even arrest him, they'll just question him and then he'll be free to do whatever he wants and he'll know it was us that sent the police to his door.'

He's right.

'How much does he want? Just pay him.'

'He doesn't want money. He wants information. Inside information that will be worth millions to him because he can sell it on. But once I give it to him, that's it, I won't be able to stop because he'll have that over me. I'll be the one taking all the risks and if I get caught, I'll be the one going to prison. I'll never be free of him.'

'There must be something we can do. There must be.'

'We have a couple of weeks breathing space, because he wants information on a big merger and it's still in the finalising stage. We've got to think of something, but we can't risk the police, Nat, no way. Even if by some chance they believed me, he's got people everywhere; the police, the courts, everywhere. Someone will tip him off. He warned me if I go anywhere near the police, there'll be no mercy.'

I wrap my arms around him and pull him towards me.

'It won't come to that,' I say, choking back the tears as the enormity of our situation sinks in. 'We'll figure something out and get through this together. We can run away, start a new life somewhere else.'

'Sounds easy, Nat, but he'd track us down. Do you want to live our life on the run, looking over our shoulders for the rest of our lives? I don't, because that wouldn't even be a life.'

I've done it already; lived a lie. I don't want to do it again.

'I don't care about what happens to me, it's you I care about.'

'Don't say that. Nothing's going to happen to either of us. We'll get through this.'

'No, you don't understand. It's not me who's in danger. He'll *hurt the thing I love,* that's what he said. He means you, it's you he'll come after.'

CHAPTER SEVENTEEN

I've run for miles this week; it's the only thing keeping me sane. As I pound around the lake for the fourth day in a row, I wonder if I'll ever have peace of mind again.

But did I ever have it? No, not completely.

Fen messaged me this morning. She said she was so looking forward to Saturday and couldn't wait to see us both again. I laughed when I read it, actually laughed. As the sound of my laughter echoed around our empty kitchen, I imagined Fen typing the message with Darius looming over her, telling her what she had to say. Does he actually think that we're going to sit and have dinner with them as if we're friends?

Fen asked if we both liked salmon as she was planning the menu. I thought about it for a while and then messaged her back and said that we loved fish, even though Brett can't stand it. I also put that we both couldn't wait to see them, too. We aren't going, but she doesn't need to know that yet.

Darius doesn't need to know yet, either.

No way are we going to sit at a table and eat with a killer.

We have three days to figure something out; three days to find a way out of an impossible situation.

I'm still trying to get my head around it. Murder, blackmail, these are things that happen in books and movies, not real life. Not my life. If it wasn't so utterly terrifying, it would be comical. My neighbour, the hitman.

Once Brett had told me everything, I studied the message with the woman's name repeatedly, looking for a way Darius could have fooled us. At first, I was sure that there must be some way he could have tricked us. Faked the date on the news article or even faked the article itself. I Googled the woman's name and countless articles in other newspapers came up in the search results, all with the same date. The texts aren't fake. There were no witnesses to the murder and the police have appealed for information. What if I rang them and told them about Darius? I dismissed the idea immediately it popped into my head; I have no proof, nothing.

We're trapped.

Darius killed Helen Wenham, just to prove to Brett that he could.

Darius doesn't look like a killer, but what does a killer look like? I've witnessed his violence against Fen, a defenceless woman, and what I saw was enough to frighten me. When he opened the door after he'd assaulted Fen, there was a moment when I was scared of him — when I was conscious of the violence in him. When Brett said that he'd come after me; I felt actual fear. If he can pick a woman at random and murder her, why not murder me? He can beat his own wife so he's going to have no qualms about a neighbour he's met a handful of times.

Although he may have known Helen Wenham; we have no way of knowing but we're hardly going to ask him.

We can't go to the police and I'll admit, the thought of Darius carrying out his threat to kill me has kept me awake at night. Brett has resigned himself to feeding him insider information and giving him what he wants. There is no other way out of this because if he doesn't do it, he's putting me in danger. He's continuing going to work as normal because what else can he do? He thinks that if he's careful, he'll get away with it and says there's no point in talking around in circles anymore. He's going to do what Darius wants. He knows as well as I do that it's only a matter of time before he gets caught giving Darius insider information. When that happens, he'll go to prison.

Our life, as we know it, will be over.

And Fen, what about her? Does she know what Darius does to people?

I want to believe that she doesn't because she's one of the gentlest people I know. I don't want to believe that she could live and share a bed with someone who kills people for money. Surely if she knew, she'd have left him.

But does she have a choice?

Most likely not; I've witnessed Darius's brutality towards her, and she will have no choice but to do as he says. Who knows what else goes on behind closed doors? I think Fen is probably just as much a prisoner to him as we are. Despite our own predicament, I can't help pitying Fen.

I saw Darius yesterday when I was returning from my run. As I ran along the street towards our house, he was in his car, pulling into their driveway. He saw me and gave a cheery wave and his trademark wide grin, but I couldn't bring myself to respond. I ran straight by without turning my head, pretending that I hadn't seen him.

How can he be so false when he's blackmailing Brett and threatening to kill me?

He's a psychopath.

A few raindrops land on my face, and I know it will soon become a deluge. The sky is low and black and the wind is picking up. I reluctantly change direction and head towards the park exit; much as I would like to, I cannot run forever.

By the time I reach my front door, the rain

is lashing down and my hair is dripping wet and plastered to my head and my clothes are soaked. I stumble into the house, splashing water everywhere, and close and double-lock the front door. I stand on the doormat and ease my feet out of my sodden trainers and peel off my socks, leaving them on the doormat in a puddle.

I run up the stairs and straight through into the ensuite. Stripping off the sopping clothes that are stuck to my skin, I throw them into the sink and turn on the shower. I step underneath the flow of hot water and stand there while it warms me.

It's sheer bliss. As I lather my hair, I attempt, once again, to tell myself that Brett is right; we have to do what Darius says. If we do as he says, our lives can continue as normal. As well as trying to convince me, Brett is trying to convince himself. He's an honest person and insider trading goes against everything he believes in. Brett knows that once he's taken that first step, Darius will have him for life.

But he has us anyway.

I wish that there was something else we could do, some way we could get rid of Darius, but if there is a way, I don't know what it is. Brett says that I need to stop trying to think of a way out and accept that we have no choice. Once I accept there's nothing we can do, it'll be easier, he says.

I hate that Darius has this power over us and the worst-case scenario part of me can't help asking; what if he wants more? What if inside information isn't enough? What will he demand next?

I hate Darius. So much.

I rinse my hair, turn off the shower and get out and briskly towel myself dry. Wrapping the towel around myself and another turban-like around my head, I go into the dressing room. I pull out fresh underwear from the chest of drawers and take clean clothes out of the wardrobe.

Brett's words are echoing around in my head, and I reluctantly accept that we have no choice. We must do as Darius demands and carry on with life. Pretend it's not happening. We can put the house up for sale, move away so that at the very least, we won't ever have to see Darius's face again.

I resolve not to think about it anymore and go into the bedroom, forcing myself to think about what I'm going to cook for dinner tonight, because that's what I have to do, think normal thoughts. I stop dead in my tracks; the clothes tumbling from my arms onto the floor.

Darius is lying on the bed. Our bed. As if he has a perfect right to be there; one leg is stretched casually over the other and he's propped up on my pillow, both arms behind his head.

'Hi, Nat.' He grins.

I gawp at him and wrap my arms around my body, gripping the towel tightly to prevent it from slipping.

'How did you get in?' The words come out in a whisper.

'Very easily. Houses are simple to get into when

you know how. You really should rethink your security, perhaps get an alarm, a few cameras, even. Not that it will stop me, but it might deter a common burglar. It's not the first time I've been in. Although usually I visit when no one is home.'

He roars with laughter, as if he's made a hilarious joke. I stand motionless, speculating if I can run fast enough to get through the bedroom doorway and down the stairs before he can catch me. How long will it take me to unlock the front door? Too long; I double-bolted it.

'You're wondering if you can escape? Get out of the house before I can stop you. I'll save you the bother of deciding; you won't. And even if you got out, what would you do? Where would you go? I think we've already established that you're not going to the police, haven't we? Because Brett will have told you what will happen if you do.'

I grip the towel even tighter and use all of my self-control to stop myself from shivering.

'He's told you everything, hasn't he?' He shakes his head and sighs. 'Disappointing. I thought he'd be a man, not go running to wifey.'

'What do you want, Darius?'

'A little chat.' He sits up and pats the mattress next to him. 'Now, come and sit next to me. You and I need to get a few things straight.'

I shake my head, unable to speak.

'I don't ask twice, Nat.' He studies me for a moment before patting the mattress again. He's no longer grinning.

On legs that feel like jelly, I move towards the bed and lower myself onto the end of the mattress. After a moment, he moves down the bed until he's sitting on the edge, next to me. I smell citrus and I guess it's his aftershave and there's a coldness about him, as if he's just come in from outdoors. I stare at his feet stretched out in front of him, his immaculately polished black shoes, and wonder if he's going to kill me and how he's going to do it.

'So, Nat, the thing is…' His fingers are on my back, moving along the top of the towel. 'I get the feeling you don't like me anymore, after everything Brett has told you.'

I feel his fingers slide down the back of the towel and tug it. I grip the front of it tightly, refusing to let it drop. He lifts his hand and takes hold of my face, gripping my chin and turning my face towards him. I have no choice but to look at him.

'That's better. For a moment there, I thought you didn't like me anymore because you ignored me when I saw you in the street, didn't you? I gave you a nice wave and a smile and you blanked me. Very rude. Impolite.'

He saw me. I curse myself for being so stupid; what did I think I was achieving by refusing to acknowledge him?

'I don't like rudeness. So unnecessary. It makes me angry.'

He stares at me, frowning, and I try to convince myself that he won't kill me, not yet, not while he still wants Brett to get his information. If he kills me now, he'll have no leverage.

'Sorry.' My mouth is so dry that my voice sounds hoarse.

He smiles.

'Good. Now we understand each other. Encourage Brett to do what he has to do, and everything will be okay. I will allow you both to continue your lives as before. Although I'm disappointed in him; I thought he would be a man and deal with it himself, instead of burdening you with it. He should have spared you. It shows his weakness, don't you think?'

I don't answer.

'He's not like you, Natalie. You're strong, I can tell. I don't think you'll tell him I've been here. There's no need for him to know about this visit, is there?' He raises an eyebrow at me and I shake my head.

'Good. It'll be our secret.' I feel the towel yanked from underneath my shoulder blade and I close my eyes. The air hits my skin as the towel falls onto the bed as Darius roughly pulls it away. He takes his hand from my face and I feel the icy touch of his fingers as he slowly unclenches my fingers from the front of the towel. I feel dizzy and barely able to breathe. I keep my eyes tightly closed as if it will help.

It doesn't.

'Hmm…very nice. Brett's a lucky man.' His fingers trail down between my breasts until he reaches my navel where they stop. He rests his hand flat on my stomach and I freeze, unable to move. 'I think maybe, that if Brett doesn't behave and do as he's told, killing you would be a waste.'

I sit rigidly, my eyes closed.

'Look at me.' He demands. His breath is on my face and I open my eyes and stare straight into his cold, dark eyes, which are only inches from mine. My insides feel as if they've turned to water. A whimper escapes me.

Transfixed by his eyes, I feel sudden, searing pain as he roughly grabs my bare breast and digs his nails into the flesh. I hold my breath and try not to cry as he twists his fingers.

'Brett will do as he's told or you will suffer.' His voice is calm and measured. 'I won't kill you; I'll keep you alive because I will have fun with you. For a while. I'll pass you on when I've finished; when I'm bored with you. I'll get a good price for you. There are many rich men who can use a woman like you. You will disappear, Natalie, and Brett will never see you again. Your life as you know it will be over, it will no longer be your own. Do you understand me?'

'Yes,' I whisper.

'Good.' He smiles. 'Now we understand each other.'

CHAPTER EIGHTEEN

Has he gone, or is he trying to trick me?

I try to estimate how long it is since he left the bedroom, but I have no idea. My brain won't work. In my terror, I've lost all sense of time; it could be hours or mere seconds since Darius left. I'm lying naked on the carpet curled into the foetal position, my arms wrapped around my legs with my face buried in my knees.

And I'm cold, so cold. I don't think I'll ever be warm again.

Stretching out my hand, I try to grab the towel, which is in a heap on the floor in front of the bed. I feel the softness of the pile beneath my fingers, but I can't seem to grasp hold of it. My fingers, like my brain, won't work. I take a deep breath and stare at the towel. Concentrate, you can do this. I focus all of my energy on taking hold of the towel and, after several attempts, I grasp a handful of cloth and drag it across the carpet towards me. I pull it awkwardly over my body with one hand, unwilling to release my other arm from around my legs. At last I feel the soft fibres of the towel on my skin and a hint of warmth returns to my body.

There's a noise. What was it?

My heart races and I brace myself; any second now he'll walk back into the room. I'm so afraid of what he might do to me.

I'm a coward.

There is no noise; only silence, save for the sound of my rapid breathing and the pounding of my heart. I inhale a deep, shuddering breath and try to calm myself. If I don't get a grip and stop panicking, I won't be able to hear or do anything.

Maybe he really has gone. I need to move; lying here, terrified, achieves nothing. My clothes and underwear are in the doorway where I dropped them. If I can make myself move, I can put them on. I'll feel better with clothes on. More in control. I push away the memory of Darius's fingers biting into my flesh.

Bury it, because thinking about it won't help.

I focus on the clothes. Get up, Nat, get up and put them on.

But I can't make myself move. My limbs simply won't obey.

I lie immobile underneath the towel, tears falling onto the carpet. Am I going to lie here until Brett comes home from work and finds me?

Do I want him to find me like this?

No. It would destroy him.

The image of Brett's reaction at seeing me like this forces me to move. I let go of my legs and stretch them. My calves immediately spasm with cramp, but I ignore it and force myself up onto all fours. I crawl painfully along the carpet towards my clothes, stopping several times to pause and listen. At last, I'm close enough to reach out and pick them up. I pull them towards me and lie on the floor and tug my knickers over my feet and up my legs and once they're on, I feel better. I slip my arms through the straps of my bra but my fingers won't work; they refuse to do up the hooks on the back. I make myself sit up and resort to doing the bra up at the front and twisting it around my waist. The material touches my breast as I pull up the bra cups and I wince. I don't look, but I know there will be a bruise there, possibly even blood. There will be time to find out later.

I hope. As long as Darius doesn't come back and find me.

I don't take my eyes away from the doorway as I dress, alert to any sound from downstairs. My fingers are clumsy and shaking as I pull on my trousers. It's as if I'm trying to dress myself wearing boxing gloves.

Once dressed, I feel marginally better, no longer naked and exposed.

I try not to feel ashamed of my weakness for allowing him to treat me the way he did. I don't let myself imagine what will happen to me if Brett doesn't do what Darius asks. The thought of disappearing into the dark underworld and being sold to the highest bidder makes me shake. There is no doubt in my mind that Darius would do it. I wish I was braver and had fought back and stopped him from touching me.

I'm weak.

Run.

The thought is there, in my head, uninvited, before I can stop it. I allow myself a moment to think about it, because it is, after all, only a thought. I could make a new identity for myself, a new life, because I've done it before. I could do it again. Yes, I could run away. Somewhere far away where Darius will never find me.

And Brett. I'd be running away from Brett.

I couldn't do it, of course. I love Brett, and there's no way I could leave him. Besides, Darius would find me because Wendy found me easily enough.

I need to concentrate on the here and now, not think of wild, foolish plans for escape.

Get up, Nat, get up.

Pulling myself to my feet, I get up from the floor as if I were eighty-years-old. It takes several attempts and my legs are wobbly when I'm upright, my head fuzzy with the sudden movement, but I did it. I sit on the edge of the bed to steady myself and take several deep breaths before I attempt any more movement.

When I'm positive he's gone, I'll change the

sheets on the bed. They're contaminated by him. I'll never be able to look at that bedding again without thinking of the moment I came out of the bathroom and saw him.

I'll throw them away. No, I'll burn them.

I need to go downstairs.

He could be down there.

No, he's gone. Why would he bother to play games with me? He's achieved what he came here to do. I get up from the bed and walk slowly to the doorway and then out onto the landing.

Silence.

I stand at the top of the stairs and listen. A noise makes me jump, but it's the sound of rain spattering against the landing window. It's raining again. I put my hand on the banister and step down onto the first step, and then slowly and quietly make my way down the stairs. Halfway down, I realise I should have looked for some sort of weapon to take with me. I'm too afraid to go back upstairs now because it's taken all of my courage to get this far. I'm not sure I have it in me to do it again. If I go back, I might lock myself in the ensuite and curl up in a ball and stay there.

Besides, what is there upstairs that I could use as a weapon?

Nothing, there is nothing I could use against him. I can hardly overpower him with a pillow. Realistically, I couldn't overpower him at all and even if I had a weapon, he could easily use it against me. I continue down the stairs until I reach the hallway. My trainers and socks are still on the doormat where I left them, a dark stain of water around them.

How did Darius get in?

It might have been the back door or the internal door from the garage. Not that it matters. Whatever locks we have didn't stop him. He found a way in easily; he said so. Creeping along the hallway; I pause when I reach the entrance to the lounge. Carefully peering around the doorframe, my breath held, I see the room is deserted and looks the same as it always does. I continue towards the kitchen and as I get closer, it looks empty. Darius is gone, unless he's hiding behind the door. I dash into the kitchen and wait for him to jump out at me; imagining his grin and laughter at fooling me.

He's not there.

The worktops are as pristine and tidy as they were before I left the house for my run, the empty coffee pot still upside down on the drainer where I put it to dry. I walk to the centre island, the tiles cold beneath my feet.

That's when I see it.

The door to the utility room is open and as I look through, I see that the internal door to the garage is ajar.

That's how he got in.

I have to close it. Even though it won't stop him from getting in again, that fact that it's open is taunting me. I'm heading towards the utility when a noise from behind shatters the silence, a noise so loud that I physically jump. My heart hammers in my chest and I think that this is it, I must surely be having a heart attack. In that moment, I believe I'm going to die until I realise.

The noise is my mobile phone ringing.

I turn and there it is on the worktop, the screen flashing. I walk towards it and slowly pick it up, dreading whose name I'm going to see on the screen.

It's Wendy.

I breathe a huge sigh of relief and press the button to take the call.

'Holly, it's Wendy. How are you?' She sounds cheerful, happy. Normal. A part of me thinks I should correct her; I'm no longer Holly, I'm Natalie now.

I don't.

I burst into tears.

And tell her everything.

✳ ✳ ✳

It helped to tell Wendy; I knew, even after all these years, that I could trust her totally. I told her everything, the dead woman, what Brett has to do.

The visit from Darius.

She didn't interrupt, but listened as I unburdened myself. It was only when I'd finished that she started talking, asking questions, but most of all, wanting reassurance that I was okay. I told her I was, but I was trying to convince myself. As we were talking, I went out into the utility room and into the garage. The electric roller door on the garage was closed and locked and I couldn't see how Darius could have got in.

Unless he has a key.

Even though it was pointless, I locked the internal door to the utility room behind me and went through to the lounge to talk to Wendy. I stood at the lounge window as we talked, and the relief I felt when I saw Darius drive away from his house and down the street was almost overwhelming. For the first time in hours, I could relax and think about what had happened without hyperventilating.

Wendy didn't suggest that I go to the police; she comes from the same place that I do; she knows exactly what people like Darius are capable of. After I'd told her everything, I didn't feel relieved, but I felt calmer and more in control; especially when I told her about Darius's visit and what he did.

I could be honest with Wendy.

I don't know if I can with Brett, because I think it might destroy him.

Should I tell him? I asked Wendy, because I needed someone to tell me what to do. She replied immediately.

No.

It wouldn't achieve anything and would probably make things worse; Brett would feel compelled to confront Darius, and while I love Brett dearly, he's no match for him. Darius wouldn't fight fair, and I feel sick when I think about what he could do to Brett. Darius may be lying, of course. He could tell Brett about his visit today himself just to mock him.

That's a risk I'll have to take.

By the time Wendy and I have finished talking, the light is fading. I haven't found a solution to the threat of Darius, but there is the faintest glimmer of one. Nothing concrete but a feeling that there is a light at the end of the tunnel. As we say our goodbyes, Wendy says something that I need to remember, something that I must repeat to myself when I'm most afraid and fearing the worst. Something that will help me.

You'll figure something out. You're the strong one, Hol, you always were.

I promise to call her soon to let her know that I'm okay and we say our goodbyes and I press the end call button. Brett will leave work soon and start his walk to the station. He'll ring me on his way, as he always does, and then he'll be home.

I need to pull myself together, otherwise he'll guess that something has happened.

I tuck my mobile phone into my pocket and hurry out to the kitchen. Walking straight across the room to the knife block, I remove the large cook's knife from it and take it with me. I go upstairs and into our bedroom and, with the knife still in my hand, I close the bedroom door. Pulling the chair out from the dressing table, I drag it over to the door and wedge the back of it underneath the handle. It won't stop Darius from getting in, but it will delay him and give me warning that he's here. I place the knife on the dressing table where it's within easy reach and strip the duvet cover, sheet, and pillowcases from the bed. I wrap them in a tight bundle and push them inside one pillowcase. They'll be going in the dustbin. I really want to burn them, but realistically, that's not possible because Brett would ask questions. Darius has tainted them forever, and I never want to look at them again. I remake the bed with fresh sheets before picking up the knife and going into the ensuite.

The wet clothes that I took off after my run are still lying in the sink; it seems years, not hours ago, that I was last in this bathroom. I take them out of the sink and toss them into the laundry basket. They're still wet, but it doesn't seem to matter now.

I shut the bathroom door and lock it. The lock is flimsy and a good kick from the other side would open the door, but at least it would slow him down if he came back. Taking the knife into the shower with me, I prop it on the shelf next to the shampoo, within easy reach. I strip off my clothes and leave them in a heap on the floor, ready for the dustbin. I'll never wear them again. I turn on the shower and step underneath the hot water and stand there as the water cascades over me. Even though it's still damp from my earlier shower, I wash my hair again. I scrub myself all over and rinse, and then repeat the process, this time using the nail brush to scrub my skin. Even when my skin is red from scrubbing, I continue. I stay in the shower for so long that the water runs cold and I force myself to stay underneath the freezing spray, pausing now and then to listen for any noise.

Nothing.

Having the knife makes me feel braver even though I know Darius could easily use it against me. He's much bigger and stronger than I am and it will be impossible for me to do him any sort of damage at all unless I'm extremely lucky. I shudder at the thought of what he could do to me with the knife. I'm probably making things much worse for myself if he should get into the house again.

I know this, and I don't care.

Because I've decided.

I'm not giving up without a fight.

CHAPTER NINETEEN

I behaved as if nothing was wrong when Brett rang me on his way to the station last night.

When he arrived home, I continued to behave as if today had been the same as any other day; as if the visit from Darius had never happened. It felt as if I was watching someone else talking to Brett instead of me. As if I wasn't really there. I'm guessing that I was in some sort of shock and it was my way of coping with it all. There's also the fact that I should be pretty good at pretending by now because I lived a lie for over twenty years.

Brett is doing the same sort of thing. He's behaving as if the Darius situation isn't happening and now doesn't want to talk about it. We've barely touched on the subject since Monday and now, if I broach it, he shuts down the conversation by saying that he's decided and it's useless to keep going over old ground. As far as he's concerned, there is no way out and he'll do what Darius says. I can't blame him for that because what can we do? It's not as if there's a manual on the correct way to behave when your neighbour starts to blackmail and threaten you.

Not telling Brett about the visit from Darius was the right decision. Like me, Brett is hanging onto his sanity by his fingertips and if I told him, I know that he'd feel compelled to do something. Violence towards Darius being the most probable course of action. That would be the very worst thing he could do because Darius was prepared to kill a woman just to prove what he was capable of, so nothing is off-limits to him. Brett is no coward, but Darius is much bigger and more powerful and utterly ruthless. Brett would be no match for him. Selfishly, the thought of what would happen to me was also behind my decision. If something happened to Brett and he was no further use to Darius, where would that leave me? Darius would have no reason to spare me, then.

I'm trying not to think about what the future holds for me if Darius carries out his threat of making me disappear. Every time my mind veers towards the thought of being sold to the highest bidder and trapped in a half-life where I'm treated as a slave, I shut it down.

It doesn't bear thinking about.

So now Brett and I are living in a weird make-believe world where, on the surface, everything is just the same as it ever was, even though it's most definitely not. We eat our meals, watch TV and chat about trivia whilst ignoring the enormous elephant in the room called Darius.

When we went to bed last night, Brett didn't know that I had the kitchen knife in my bedside table drawer. I added a can of hairspray to the drawer to use as a weapon; a blast of that in Darius's eyes would give me valuable time to get away.

I lay awake and relived yesterday, whilst Brett snored beside me. Every minute from the moment I came out of the bathroom until he finally left, replayed in my head, over and over, on a loop. Even if I could have forgotten, my breast would have reminded me as it was so sore that if I moved, it hurt. As well as a black and purple bruise, there are several painful cuts where his fingernails broke the skin. Whilst I lay awake replaying it, I had the same feelings of dread and fear that I experienced when it happened, but there was something else, too.

Anger.

He's ruining our lives and making us do what he wants and has total control of us. There is no way out of the situation. I feel rage at him for making us afraid for the rest of our lives, afraid of what he might do to us.

There's no way we can have a family now. A child would be someone else Darius could threaten; how could we ever have children knowing he could take them away whenever he chose? They would never be safe. We can't plan for the future or do anything because he's there, ready to destroy us at any given moment. And what if Brett gets caught? Byersons will make sure he gets a prison sentence. They'll make an example of him to ensure that no employee even *thinks* about stealing from them again. Prison will finish Brett; his life will be over. And after he's released, he'll never get a job in the city again.

If Brett goes to prison, what happens to me? Will Darius leave me be when his personal financial insider can no longer feed him information? Not for one second do I believe he will. He will use me, abuse me and sell me to the highest bidder and there's nothing I could do to stop it. I could go to the police because there'll be nothing to lose if Brett were in prison, but I'm sure Darius would get to me before I had the chance to do so.

By the time dawn broke this morning, I'd barely had a wink of sleep. But I felt the first stirrings of hope, because I'd spent those dark hours thinking of a way out of this mess. I'd formulated a plan, of sorts, but for it to work, I need help.

Brett didn't know that I'd lain awake all night, although he did comment that I looked tired as we ate our breakfast together. I waved him off to work and when he'd gone; I cleared away the breakfast dishes as if it were a normal day. After showering, I got dressed in my running gear, keeping the knife and hairspray with me every step of the way.

Once dressed, I went downstairs and put on my dried out trainers and laced them up, but I didn't go out; I went into the lounge and sat in the chair nearest the window. From that vantage point I had a perfect view of Fen and Darius's house and driveway. If anyone left that house today, either in a car or on foot, I'd be able to see them.

I put my feet up on the pouffe, and I waited.

* * *

The warmth of the room and lack of sleep last night makes me drowsy and my eyelids heavy. The pull of sleep is so irresistible that I almost miss Darius's car pulling off the driveway and into the street. For a second, I think that I'm dreaming, but in that trance-like moment before I plunge headlong into slumber, I remember why I'm sitting here.

I leap out of the chair and watch his black BMW zoom off down the road and disappear around the corner. Wasting no time, I hurry to the hallway, take my keys from the bowl on the console table, and open the front door. I step outside, pull the front door closed behind me, and then jog across the street to Fen and Darius's house. I scan the road as I cross to make sure Darius hasn't changed his mind and is on his way back. The road is empty and I jog through the open gates to their house.

I run down the driveway with a sense of urgency and straight up the steps onto their porch without stopping. Standing at their front door, I press the button for the bell before I can change my mind and keep my finger on it. I can't hear the bell out here, but Fen won't be able to ignore the shrill ringing that it makes inside the house.

I pray that I'm right about Fen, because if I'm not, I'm dead.

Or worse.

My heart is pounding and I have a sudden urge to go to the toilet, but I take a deep breath and keep my finger pressed firmly on the button.

Answer the door, Fen.

Please.

A shadow is coming down the hall, growing closer, the outline blurred through the opaque glass. I have a sudden irrational thought that it's Darius, that he's tricked me into believing he's left the house and I've walked right into the trap that he's set.

No, the shadow's not big enough, it *can't* be him. It's not him. It's not.

I remove my finger from the button and after what seems like forever, Fen pulls open the door.

'Hello Nat, how lovely to see you.'

She's smiling, but she can't hide her surprise or the hint of wariness in her eyes.

'Can I come in?' I didn't mean for the words to come out so bluntly; I sound gruff and desperate.

'Oh, of course.' She moves aside and I stand motionless for a moment before stepping inside. The fear of Darius coming back is overwhelming, but I force myself onwards.

I have to do this; I remind myself. I have no choice.

'Come through to the kitchen.' Fen walks down the hall. 'I'll make us a drink.'

Following behind her, once we reach the kitchen, I climb up onto the same stool that I sat on the first time I came here. The first day we met, when I yearned to be her friend.

A lifetime ago.

'Tea or coffee?'

'Neither, thank you. How long will Darius be out?' I ask, bluntly.

She's silent as she studies me, and I stare back at her.

What if I've got it wrong? I've sealed my fate by coming here. She's in it with Darius; she knows what he does and she'll keep me here until he returns.

My life is over.

I should have run while I had the chance.

'A couple of hours, maybe more,' she eventually says. 'He has some important business to attend to in town. What's wrong, Nat? Is there something you need to speak to him about?'

She's not smiling now.

'No, I don't want to speak to him. I wanted to make sure he won't come back while I'm here.'

Silence. She's not even asking why.

'Sit down, Fen. I have things to tell you about Darius. Bad things.'

A coolness creeps into her expression; a

shutting down of the Fen I've come to know in our brief friendship.

'I think you'd better leave,' she says.

'I saw him, Fen. The day I came round with the flowers, I saw what he did to you. I know what sort of man he is and the way he treats you.'

'I don't know what you're talking about.' She's already walking towards the hallway. 'You need to go now.'

'I looked through the lounge window that day to see if you were in, Fen. I saw him pushing you around. He hits you, too, doesn't he? Is that why you always wear long sleeves and trousers, to hide the bruises? Is that what the polo necks are for?' Until I uttered the words, I hadn't realised, but it's true; Fen's always covered up. It doesn't look strange now because it's winter, but what does she do in the summer?

Her usually pale complexion flushes red as she turns away from me and walks down the hallway to the front door.

'Please Fen, let me help you. You shouldn't have to live like this.'

She's already at the door and she shakes her head, refusing to look at me as she fumbles with the lock.

'Please,' she says. 'Just go. Now. Before it's too late and he comes back.' She puts her hand on the door handle to open it and I quicken my step to stop her.

'Fen...' I put my hand on hers, to prevent her

from opening the door, but she shakes my hand off, surprising me with her strength.

'Just GO Nat. You don't know what you're talking about. You can't help me, no one can.' She turns the handle and opens the door, but I put both of my hands on it and shove it closed. She looks at me in shock.

'I know. I know *exactly* what he's capable of.'

We're standing so close together I can feel her breath on my face and we stare into each other's eyes. She drops her gaze and takes her hand from the lock. She looks beaten and exhausted and despite my fears for myself, my heart goes out to her.

'We can help each other, Fen.'

She's silent for a moment.

'Okay.' She straightens her shoulders and then turns and walks down the hallway and through the doorway into the lounge. I check the front door to make sure it's locked and then follow her.

'Let's sit over here.' She lowers herself into the chair nearest the window. 'I can watch the street from here. I'll see him if he comes back and you can leave by the back door if he does. There's a gate at the end of the garden that leads onto the back of the park. He doesn't even know it's there, it's behind the summerhouse. He'll never know you've been here.'

I sit down on the sofa opposite her, grateful to have an escape route should I need one.

'He's threatening us,' I say. 'If Brett doesn't

feed him insider financial information from his company, then I'm dead. Or worse.'

She closes her eyes and nods her head.

'Did you know?' I demand. 'Did he tell you?'

She opens her eyes and looks at me.

'No. He rarely tells me anything unless he's in a bragging mood. I didn't know. But it's not a surprise, it's what he does. You're not the first and you won't be the last. I'm sorry, Nat, we should never have become friends and then he might have left you alone. I'd hoped that he would, but I should have known. He can't resist an opportunity.'

'An opportunity?' I demand. 'Is that how you see us, as an opportunity?'

She shakes her head. 'Of course not. They're Darius's words, not mine. I'm truly sorry. I wish there was something I could do, but there isn't. Do as he asks, Nat, and he'll be true to his word. Don't cross him and all will be well.'

'No! I want my life back. I don't want to do what he says. How can you stay with someone like him and let him treat you this way? How can you live with him knowing what he does to people?'

'You have to ask me that? You think I *want* to stay? I hate him, Nat, probably much more than you do.'

'I doubt it,' I mutter.

'Don't doubt it.' She looks out of the window, checking the driveway. 'He hates me, too. That's why he won't let me leave, because he enjoys making me suffer. It amuses him to see me in pain and, of course, I'm useful for sex. You have to understand that Darius is not like us, he has a piece missing, Nat, in his brain, the piece that makes us all human. He doesn't have it. You cannot appeal to his better nature because he doesn't have one. He fooled me when we first met, just as he fooled you and Brett, but it's too late for me now. There is no escape from him. One day he will kill me or make me disappear.'

'I don't know how you do it, how you stay with him.'

'I have no choice.'

'There's always a choice.'

'No, there isn't. He would find me. He's good at finding people, but he knows I would never leave him. I have a sister, a nephew. I have to stay with him for their sakes.'

'You don't have to stay,' I say.

'I do. If I leave him, he's promised me he will kill them.'

'You don't have to leave him,' I repeat. 'If he was dead, he wouldn't be able to find you. Ever. You, your sister, your nephew, all of us would be safe.'

'Dead?'

'Yes. If Darius was dead, he could never come after us. We'd be free. We wouldn't have to spend the rest of our lives looking over our shoulders.'

'Oh Nat, don't you think I've thought of that, of killing him? Because I have, many, many times. But I'm not strong enough to kill him.' She shakes her

head. 'I wish I was.'
   'I am.'
   'What?'
   'I'll kill him,' I say. 'If you help me.'

CHAPTER TWENTY

'You're shitting me.'

Brett stares at me, his mouth set in a straight line.

'No,' I say. 'I am not.'

He sighs, rakes his fingers through his hair, rests his head in his hands and stares down at the table for several minutes before looking up at me. We've just finished breakfast and are still sitting at the table in the kitchen.

'So, let me get this right, because I think I might have just stepped into a parallel universe. We're expected to have dinner tonight with our neighbours across the street and behave as if we're not being blackmailed and extorted by one of them?'

I hold my hands up in surrender. 'Don't shoot the messenger, I'm just reading you the message

Fen sent. I didn't write it. I'm as surprised as you are.'

He glares at me and waggles his fingers at me impatiently, wanting me to give him my mobile phone. I pass it over and wait while he reads the message that Fen sent me this morning. I read it out to him mere moments ago, and it wasn't very long, so he can't have forgotten it.

Hi! We're so looking forward to seeing you for dinner tonight. Darius has a special bottle of limited edition brandy he can't wait to share with Brett. X

Brett tosses the phone onto the worktop with a clatter and sighs.

'We have to get out of it. I'm not sitting at the same table as him.

'Okay. I'll message her and say one of us is ill. Pretend I've got a stomach bug or something.'

We face each other across the table without speaking. Brett knows as well as I do that we'll be going to dinner with them. All this talk about not going is just that; talk. Darius is expecting us to go and to make an excuse and to not turn up would be the worst thing we could do. When Darius says jump, you ask how high, not try to wriggle out of it with feeble excuses. He's unpredictable and a violent bully. No way are we going to turn him down. Brett is venting his feelings, but he knows as well as I do that we're going, like it or not.

'Oh, what's the point?' Brett jumps up from the chair, snatches his cereal bowl from the table, and carries it to the sink, dumping it in with a clatter.

'We both know we don't have any fucking choice. He owns us now, every bit of us, and we have to do whatever he says.'

It's true. But that's not the only reason we have to go; if we don't go tonight, my plan won't work.

'We can do it,' I say. 'We can pretend for the evening, pretend that they're really our friends. It's just one night, Brett, a few hours of faking.'

'It's not though, is it?' He demands. 'Because we'll have to do this whenever he decides he wants our company. We're trapped. Forever. From now on, he runs our lives and tells us what to do.'

Tonight will be the one and only night if my plan works, but Brett doesn't know that because I haven't told him anything about it. If it doesn't work, it'll be the last night that the four of us will ever be together because I'll be dead; or Darius will have made me disappear.

'Let's take it one step at a time,' I say. 'Get tonight over with and not worry about the next time. It'll be easier to cope with that way. There's no point fretting about the future.'

Brett doesn't answer. I need tonight to happen.

'We could make sure we bore the arse off him and then he won't want us there ever again.' I'm trying for a bit of humour here.

'I'll have to get pissed.'

I laugh, lightening the moment. 'You could drink all of his limited edition brandy. Drain the bottle, that would really piss him off.'

'Yeah, I fucking will.' He walks over to stand

behind me and I feel his arms snake around my waist. 'I'll glug it back like it's water and then puke it up all over him.'

I laugh and after a moment, he joins in.

'We can do this,' I whisper as I cross my fingers underneath the table. 'We can get through tonight.'

'We can,' he says, kissing my neck as I relax back into him. 'It's just dinner, a free meal, and free booze. We can do it.'

If only it were just dinner.

I can do this.

I *have* to do this.

* * *

Brett winks at me and grins as we wait on the porch at Fen and Darius's house. Stabbing the doorbell repeatedly with his finger, he has a glint in his eye and is clearly enjoying himself. I imagine the clattering noise the bell is making inside the house. He's already drunk two large glasses of wine and the effects of it have kicked in. He poured me a large glass, too, and although I pretended to drink it, I threw it down the sink and washed it away when he went to the toilet.

I need a clear head for tonight.

Fen does too, which is why, although it'll appear as if we're drinking copious amounts of wine, we'll actually be drinking an alcohol free version which Fen will have decanted into a normal bottle.

I look up, and Darius is in front of us with the door open. He fills the doorway. Brett pretends not to notice and continues stabbing the button. The high-pitched sound is deafening now that the door is open and after a few more stabs, Brett stops and looks up at Darius with a smirk. Darius frowns at him before turning his attention to me. His eyes sweep up and down my body before settling on my face. I fight the urge to squirm under his scrutiny but keep my expression impassive. I now wish I'd drunk the wine that Brett poured me.

'Good evening!' He beams his trademark smile, and I force the corners of my mouth upwards.

'You can take your finger off the bell now, mate.' He frowns at Brett again, whose smirk is now even cheesier. 'Come on in.'

After a stony silence, I feel Brett's hand on my back as he pushes me forward.

Thanks Brett.

I step into the hallway with Brett close behind me and attempt to get past Darius. He's standing in the way and doesn't move, forcing me to try to squeeze past him.

'Good to see you.' Darius leans in to me and his lips brush my cheek. The smell of his citrus aftershave catapults me back into my bedroom with him and I have an impulse to hit him.

I don't, obviously.

Unseen by Brett, Darius puts his hand on my arm and digs his fingers in, making me wince. I pull away from him and continue into the house, and he grins and puts his hand out to Brett. Brett stares at Darius's offered hand as if a dead rat is being offered to him.

Is he going to ignore him? Take it, Brett, I silently urge, shake his hand and play the game. After what feels like hours, he puts out his arm and takes Darius's hand.

'Glad you could come, mate,' Darius says with a grin, pumping Brett's hand up and down, water-pump style.

'Likewise,' Brett mutters.

'Hey, let me take your coat for you.' Darius's hands are on my shoulders and I force myself not to flinch. I shrug my arms out of the sleeves and as he takes my coat from me, his fingers brush my breast. So casual that it could have been by accident, but I know it wasn't; it was deliberate. It's the same breast that bears the imprint of his nails and it was a warning, a reminder, of what he can do if he chooses.

'Come on through. Fen's been cooking up a storm all day. Surf and turf tonight, mate.' He grins at Brett. 'Because she knows us men like our steak.'

We follow him into the kitchen, throwing glances at each other behind his back. Brett mouths *fish* at me and pulls a disgusted face and I try not to laugh.

Wiping her hands on a towel, Fen comes out from behind the kitchen island to greet us. I hug her, and Brett steps forward and kisses her. In those few steps from the hallway, he seems to have recovered his composure and if I didn't know otherwise, I'd think that this was a perfectly normal evening.

Fen talks, meaningless chatter about the steak and where she bought it from, how the butcher selected the best cut for her, the wine we're drinking, the special brandy Darius is so desperate for Brett to try. A constant stream of inane conversation to prevent the silence that would engulf us all if she stopped.

Darius pours us all a glass of wine, showing Brett the wine label and boasting about how expensive it is. In no time at all, we're seated in the dining room and Fen is bringing in the first course. Unbelievably, we're managing to behave as if having dinner with a killer is a perfectly normal occurrence. Darius is being charming and witty, entertaining us with amusing tales of business deals he's brokered in the past. He is unrecognisable as the violent psychopath who broke into our house and terrified me.

The wine flows but my head remains clear as, unbeknown to either Brett or Darius, there is no alcohol in my wine, although I try to give the impression there is by giggling and laughing at every remotely funny remark. Fen and I are drinking white, whereas they are drinking red. Darius laughs at us for our choice of wine and wants to know why we're drinking white wine when we're eating steak. I remind him we're also eating salmon, so white is the perfect choice.

The evening is surreal and dream-like as Fen serves the dinner, and I hope that I'm the only one who notices her trembling as she spoons vegetables onto her plate. After we've finished eating, I offer to help Fen clear the table and we decamp to the kitchen, leaving Darius and Brett to enjoy their brandy. It's a relief to be away from them, and we take our time loading the dishwasher and tidying up. Perhaps because we're stone cold sober, Darius and Brett both seem to have got drunk very quickly. Darius is already slurring his words and is talking so loudly that he's almost shouting. Perhaps he was like this the last time we had dinner together; he might have been, but I never noticed because I wasn't scrutinising him in the way I am now.

At the end of the evening, when it's almost one o'clock in the morning, Fen suggests coffee. I hold my breath as I wait for Darius's answer. He *has* to have coffee. It's a vital part of the plan. Fen says he always finishes the evening with coffee, but I can't help worrying that tonight, he'll be suspicious and he won't. My fears are unfounded. He asks for his usual strong black coffee and Fen returns to the kitchen to make it.

When she returns, I can't look at her as she brings in the delicate china cups and the cafetiere of coffee that she's made. We don't want to wake them up; we want them both to sleep soundly, so the coffee is decaffeinated.

And Darius's has been spiked with crushed

sleeping tablets.

* * *

I lie in bed and listen to Brett's breathing. I have to be sure that there's no possibility of him waking up and finding my side of the bed empty. With the amount of alcohol he drank tonight, it's unlikely, even so, to be sure, I wait a little longer.

I go over everything in my mind once more whilst I wait. I need to have every detail clear, every eventuality accounted for. There is only one chance to do this.

When Brett's breathing turns into snoring, I slip out of bed, take my mobile phone from the bedside table, and pull the duvet back over my side of the bed. I make my way out of the bedroom and onto the landing, pausing outside the bedroom doorway to satisfy myself that Brett is asleep. He is; the snores don't falter. I creep down the stairs and into the hallway in the darkness. I don't turn on the lights but continue along the hallway, into the kitchen and straight through into the utility room. It's only when I get inside the utility room and have closed the door that I turn on the light. I stand still for a moment and blink while my eyes adjust to the sudden brightness and then open the tumble dryer door. I take out the clothing that I put in there earlier today; a pair of black joggers, a black sweatshirt, black trainers and a black baseball cap. I put aside the cap that's on top of the clothing to put on last. It belongs to Brett but he won't notice it's missing as he has caps galore in the hall cupboard. He rarely wears any of them except when he plays golf.

I rip off the t-shirt that I wore to bed and throw it in the tumble dryer, out of sight. I never took my underwear off when I got undressed for bed and I pull on the joggers and sweatshirt. Before slipping my feet into the trainers, I realise I don't have any socks to wear. It's too late now. I won't risk waking Brett by going upstairs to get some.

So far, so good.

I open the cupboard underneath the sink and pull out the box of laundry tablets, then remove the small black case hidden behind it. There was no possibility of Brett finding the case, as he never looks in this cupboard because I'm the one who does the washing.

The case is my samples case from when I was working as a medical representative. Strictly speaking, I should have returned the assorted drugs and syringes to the company when I left, but I, like most people, never bothered. The company doesn't really want them back because they'd have to be destroyed anyway. I was intending to take them to the local pharmacy to dispose of them myself but have never got around to it. I open the case and take out the rubber gloves that I bought at the supermarket; they're thicker than disposable gloves but thinner than washing up gloves. Pulling them onto my hands, I ease them over my fingers, flexing them to ensure I have full mobility. Once I'm satisfied they're comfortable, I take a small plastic bag out of the case. Inside are two syringes and I touch the caps on the needles through the plastic of the bag to check that they're fixed firmly in place. I drew up the contents of the bottles yesterday whilst Brett was at work to save myself from having to do it now. I was afraid that nerves might get the better of me and I didn't want any accidents. Satisfied that everything is ready, I shove the bag into my hoodie pocket and zip it closed.

When I searched the house for my samples case yesterday, I had an anguished hour when I couldn't find it. I knew I wouldn't have thrown it out —I'm not so irresponsible as to put prescription medicines and syringes into the dustbin—but I couldn't remember where I'd put it. It was only when I made myself sit down and think it through that I remembered where they were.

The garage.

I hadn't got around to taking them to the local pharmacy to dispose of them; sheer laziness, I suppose, so I'd put them somewhere safe and out of reach. They were inside a cardboard box high up on top of Brett's tool cupboard. Thank God I didn't get rid of them; without these syringes and drugs, I wouldn't have a plan.

I close the case and return it to the cupboard, placing it out of sight behind the washing powder. Taking a hair tie that's looped around my wrist, I scoop my hair up into a ponytail and double it over, bun-style, wrapping the tie tightly around it. I pull the cap on, carefully pushing the bun through the opening at the back; it's a snug fit. I give it a tug. It doesn't shift at all; the tight fit of the bun through the opening is keeping it securely fixed to my head.

Turning out the light, I open the utility door and creep across the unlit kitchen to the back door. I unlock it, take the key out, and open the door. The chilly night air hits me as I step outside and I pull the door closed behind me as silently as possible before inserting the key and locking it. I walk alongside the house until I reach the kitchen window and then stop and slip the key underneath one of the plant pots that sits there. Making no noise, I continue along the path until I reach the gate that leads into the front garden. I slip the latch to unlock it and open the gate. The creaking of the hinges as I push it open sounds loud enough to wake the dead. Should I leave it open? No; because the wind could blow the gate against the house wall, and the banging noise it would make would be far louder than the noise of the hinges.

I walk across the driveway and open one gate just wide enough to slip through onto the pavement and then pull it closed behind me. The street looks deserted, but so it should be at three o'clock in the morning. A tiny sliver of moon is just visible through thick clouds and the lamp posts throw weak illumination at intervals along the pavement.

I touch my pockets to reassure myself that I have what I need, feeling the outline of the syringes in one pocket, my phone in the other.

I take a deep breath.

I'm ready.

I can do this.

I can.

Because I've done it before.

CHAPTER TWENTY-ONE

'I can't.' Wendy sobs. 'I can't.'

I wrap my arms around her, pull her to me, and cuddle her. I can feel her shaking and I hold her tightly to stop her.

'I'm sorry.'

'It's alright, Wend, you don't have to do it, I can do it on my own. It doesn't need both of us. You stay here and I'll go in. Just give me the bag.'

She doesn't move.

'Scruffy's in there,' she whispers. 'I forgot about him. I've left him on my bed.'

I let go of her and take the carrier bag from her.

'I can't leave him to burn, Hol.' She starts to cry again.

'It's okay, don't worry. I'll get him.'

She's had Scruffy since she was a baby; he's threadbare and his paws are tatty where she holds them, but she always sleeps with him. Even on the bathroom floor. I don't want to go upstairs; I want to be in and out of the house as quickly as I can, but I'll have to get him because this is all bad enough without Wendy losing Scruffy. It'll only take a minute to run up to her bedroom and get him.

We're going to start the fire in front of the fireplace in the lounge, so it looks as if a piece of coal fell out and caught the rug alight and it got out of control. Or something like that. Wendy's mum keeps a pile of old newspapers next to the fire that she scrunches up and uses to get the fire going. We're going to put petrol on them and throw a match on them.

'I'm sorry, Hol, for being such a scaredy cat.'

'It's alright. It doesn't need both of us to do it, probably safer if it's just me that goes. I'll be in and out in a couple of minutes, and then we can go home and forget about it. You stay out here and keep watch, make sure none of your neighbours are about. Give me your key.'

She fumbles in her coat pocket and pulls out a piece of string with the back door key hanging from it.

'I won't be long.' Gripping the carrier bag tightly, I walk over to the back door. I put the key into the lock and turn it and then push the door open. Leaving the key in the lock, I go into the house and push the door closed behind me. The kitchen smells of chips and my stomach growls with hunger as I hurry past the table and chairs and out into the hallway. I go straight up the stairs and along the landing to Wendy's bedroom. It's at the back of the house and I head towards it,

passing the bathroom on my way. The bathroom door is wide open. It doesn't have a handle or a lock on it anymore and there are screw holes where it used to be. My stomach is churning with nerves, but looking at the screw holes makes me feel braver. I have to do this because Wendy can't come back here.

I go into Wendy's bedroom and go straight over to her bed. Scruffy is sitting on her pillow and I pick him up and stuff him down the front of my coat. He's got bald patches all over him and he's all flat where the stuffing has fallen out. One of his proper eyes has gone and been replaced by a black button. Wendy loves him like he's real. I look around the bedroom for one last time and then head back to the landing. I just want to get it done and get out and get home.

I have my foot on the top step of the stairs when a noise stops me in my tracks. I freeze and listen, wondering if Wendy has come into the house. She wouldn't. And anyway, the noise isn't coming from downstairs, it's coming from the front bedroom. I turn and tiptoe along the landing until I'm outside Wendy's mum's bedroom. The noise is louder here; a snorting, blowing noise. I stop and peer slowly around the doorway into the room.

Griff is in there.

I flinch at the sight of him and am backing away when I realise he doesn't know I'm here. He's asleep and the snorting noise is his snoring. I sneak back into the room and look at him, sprawled out on the bed and snoring like a pig. His thick rubber lips are gaping open, showing his grubby, jagged teeth. He's got his work clothes on and they're splattered with all different colours of paint. Still wearing his boots, the soles are caked with mud and grit, leaving big brown streaks on the bedspread. Beer bottles are scattered on the bedside table and one of them has fallen onto its side and is dripping beer onto the floor. On the floor next to the bed, there's an ashtray overflowing with dog ends.

Disgusting pig.

Why does Wendy's mum think he's so great? He's an ugly slob who can't even take his boots off before he lies on the bed. I stand and watch him for a while, thinking about how much I hate him and how stupid Wendy's mum is. He doesn't move at all, just keeps making his grunting pig noises. I back slowly out of the bedroom until I'm at the top of the stairs. I listen for one more minute to make sure his snoring doesn't stop, and then I start down the stairs.

I feel an absolute hatred for him.

I creep down the steps, trying so hard not to cry that it hurts to swallow. We can't start the fire now because he's here; he's ruined everything. I hate him even more. Why tonight? Why did he have to choose tonight to be here?

I feel panic rising; Wendy will be back home tomorrow and there's no lock on the bathroom door and she won't be able to stop him. We've planned everything for tonight and now he's wrecked it and we can't do anything. I feel sick at what he's going to do to Wendy tomorrow night when her mum's gone to work.

Once I'm downstairs, I stand in the hallway and

try to think of something I can do to keep him from hurting Wendy again. Maybe she could stay at my house again tomorrow. Dad wouldn't know. He'd have no idea she was there.

But Wendy's mum would. She's let her sleep over at mine for tonight, but she won't allow another night; she'll think we're up to something. We might be able to do it next week. She could ask her mum if she could have another sleepover. That could work.

But that's seven whole days away. Seven nights.

I turn towards the kitchen, seeing Wendy's face in my mind, remembering how she said she might as well be dead.

I stop.

I could start the fire, anyway.

My stomach flips over at the thought.

That's murder.

If I set the fire and the house burns down, Griff will die.

He deserves to die.

I stand in the hallway, with it all spinning around in my head.

And then I turn and walk towards the lounge.

✳ ✳ ✳

'Hol, stop, stop. I can't breathe, I've got a stitch.'

She doubles over, clutching her stomach, and we run into a nearby bus shelter and huddle inside. The brick built shelter stinks of wee, and empty beer bottles and cans litter one corner. They're the same as the ones next to Griff's bed and the cans are the ones like Dad drinks.

I draw a lungful of shuddering breath. We've been running since I came tearing out of the house and we haven't stopped once. I feel as if we've been running forever.

I never thought the fire would catch so quickly. In my mind, I thought the newspapers would burn for a little while and then gradually, everything else would catch fire and me and Wendy would be at my house by the time it was burning properly.

Not so.

I pushed the pile of newspapers over onto the floor and spread them out in front of the fire like we'd planned. I hoped it would look like a hot coal had fallen out of the grate and caught alight. Unscrewing the top of the can, I sprinkled the petrol over them, but my hands were shaking so much that it splashed all over the floor as well. Some went on the sofa, too. I didn't know how much to use, so I emptied it all out and then threw the can on top of the newspapers, because the fire would burn the can away to nothing, wouldn't it?

It stank so much; I felt nauseous with the fumes and thought maybe I shouldn't light the match because the air might catch fire. I was terrified that it would all go wrong, and I'd burn to death.

But I had to do it. I had no choice. There was petrol all over the room, so I couldn't just walk away and leave it. I forced myself to put my hand into my pocket and take out the matches. All you have to do is strike one match and drop it onto the newspapers, I told myself. Just do it. I opened the box, took out a match, and scraped it along the side of the box.

Nothing.

I tried again.

Nothing.

I held the match up in front of my eyes and looked at it; it was already spent. Where there should have been a fat, bulbous head, was flat charred wood. Dad does that; puts the used matches back in the box. I should have remembered that. I took out another match; that was spent, too. I was panicking by then; the smell of the petrol was overwhelming, and I thought I was going to throw up. Three more spent matches followed before I found a live one.

I struck it and it flared into life and in my panic; I dropped both the match and the box onto the floor.

The room exploded.

There was an ear-splitting whooshing noise, followed by such intense heat that I thought I must be on fire. The skin on my face felt as if it was boiling and my lungs were burning, as if they'd had all the air sucked out of them. For a second, I couldn't make my legs work and then the curtains caught fire with a ripping noise, and it spurred me into action.

I ran, pumping my legs as hard as I could.

I'm don't know how I got out of that room alive; luck, I think. I tore out into the hallway, stumbling along on legs made of jelly. Wendy had opened the back door, and I bolted straight through the kitchen and out into the garden and she slammed the door *shut behind me. As we raced down the garden, we looked back over our shoulders and could see the flames through the kitchen windows.*

And now we're here, we're safe. Wendy's safe.

'Can you hear that?' Wendy is standing upright now, holding her waist as the stitch subsides.

It's a siren. A fire engine. Several sirens. Loud, screaming, urgent.

Close.

'I forgot to take the key out of the back door,' Wendy says.

'They won't notice,' I say. 'It doesn't matter.'

'Your face is all red, Hol.'

I touch my cheek and it feels sore; like sunburn. My hands stink of petrol.

'Thank you for doing it and for getting Scruffy. I'm sorry for being a coward,' Wendy says.

'S'alright.'

'I'm sad about Mum, though. She's going to be upset about the house and all our stuff being gone.'

'But you won't have to see him again, so it'll be worth it.'

'I think Mum will still see him, 'cos she's mad about him. But she'll have to meet him somewhere else 'cos Nan won't have him in her house. She hates him, says he looks like Gollum.'

Did Griff wake up when the petrol exploded? The living room door was open, and it's right next to the bottom of the stairs, so he must have heard it. The flames were near the doorway when I came running out. Did he get out?

I don't think he did.

I hope he didn't.

'Do you think God will judge us for what we've done, Hol?'

'I don't believe in God.'

'It's only a house though, isn't it? And we had a good reason, and it's not as if we've hurt anyone.' Wendy sounds worried. I know she wants me to make her feel better. She goes to church with her nan sometimes.

'God won't judge us, Wend, but Griff will have to answer to him for what he's done.'

'He will,' Wendy says. 'Although it won't be for a long time because he's not really old yet, so he won't die for ages. I hope God hasn't forgotten all the bad things he's done by the time he dies.'

'He won't.' I promise, wondering how Wendy can believe in God after what Griff did to her. Why didn't God stop him?

'We need to go,' I say. 'Get back to mine, pretend we've been there all night.'

I haven't told her Griff was in the house; there's no need for her to know. I'll pretend to her I never saw him. I wouldn't have seen him if he hadn't been snoring like a pig.

I wish I hadn't seen him.

'I'm not bad, am I, Hol?' Wendy asks again, as we come out of the bus shelter and walk towards home. 'I won't go to hell, will I?'

'Of course you won't,' I say.

But I might.

CHAPTER TWENTY-TWO

I run down the street in the direction of the park, taking care to stay near the garden walls so that I'm not illuminated by the streetlights. Some of these houses could have security cameras and I could trigger the motion alerts and be picked up on them. There's no way I can avoid them, as I don't know which houses have them so I run with my head downwards, looking at the pavement so that the peak of the baseball cap shields my face. This will make it more difficult, if not impossible, to identify me. I wore black to blend into the darkness, but that won't help if security lights pick me up and cameras come on. No matter which way I look at it, running down the street after three o'clock in the morning looks suspicious.

I can't do anything about it so there's no point in worrying about it. Hopefully the police won't ask residents to check their security cameras because there will be no crime to investigate.

When I reach the park, I'm surprised to hear voices coming from the lake. Shouting and whooping noises shatter the silence and for a moment, I'm alarmed. Am I about to witness someone being mugged or attacked? The whooping turns to laughter and I relax. To lessen the risk of encountering anyone, I veer off the path and onto the grass. My trainers make squelching sounds as I run and I can see my breath coming out of my mouth in clouds of vapour. I race along, scanning the darkness of the trees and hedges at the edge of the park to get my bearings. In the dark it's difficult to see exactly where I am and too late, I realise I should have counted my steps or timed myself so I could judge the distance to the back entrance to Fen's house. The trees are very dense now and I slow to a jog. It has to be around here somewhere. I take my phone from my pocket and turn on the torch, covering the beam slightly with my fingers to make it less bright. I point it at the ground beneath the trees, looking for a gap.

Nothing. I jog further, but I still can't find it. Feeling unnerved and slightly panicked, I push the feelings down. It has to be here somewhere. It can't have vanished. Just calm down and find it.

The whoops and shouting sound closer and that's when I realise that I've come too far. The entrance to Fen's back garden isn't this close to the lake. I turn around and retrace my footsteps, and this time, I find the gap in the trees. I ran straight past it. Jogging through the gap, the tall brick wall that surrounds the park on this side looms up in front of me. Fen's is one of several houses with direct access to the park with gates at the rear of their gardens, although some householders have bricked them up. Fen said she'd tie something to the gate, so I'd know which one is theirs. I pass two gates, neither of them with anything tied on them, and the one after that has been bricked up. Feeling totally disorientated, I have no clear idea where I am and sense that I've missed Fen's gate and come too far. Doing a practice run during the day would have been the logical thing to do, but I was afraid of Darius catching me.

I hope Fen hasn't forgotten to put something on the gate.

Or changed her mind about what we're going to do.

No. She wouldn't do that; she's as much a prisoner as we are. She hates Darius as much, if not more, than I do.

The next gate I reach has a piece of tattered blue rope tied around the handle, and I breathe a sigh of relief. This must be the one. I turn off the torch and, as agreed, type a message to Fen.

Here.

I watch the message go and then two ticks appear.

Fen is typing...

A thumb up emoji appears followed by *door is*

unlocked.

I study the message for a few moments before clicking the screen closed. I slip the phone into my pocket and zip it up. Grasping hold of the gate handle, I push it open and step into the garden. Directly in front of me, only a foot away, are the wooden slats of the summerhouse. Pulling the gate closed, I stand behind the summerhouse, checking every detail in my head of what I have to do.

I'll get only one chance at this.

I shuffle my way along the back of the summerhouse until I emerge into the garden. There's a path down the centre and as I begin to walk down it, a spotlight springs into life, illuminating the entire garden in brilliant white light. Neither one of us had anticipated this. Feeling completely exposed and as if I'm standing in the middle of a stage, I sprint to the side of the garden and stand immobile, waiting for the spotlight to go off, guessing that it's on a movement sensor. After a long minute, it goes out, and the garden is in darkness again. I allow a few moments for my eyes to adjust and then feel my way along, sticking as close to the garden wall as possible. Their garden is enormous, much larger than ours, and it crosses my mind that they must employ a gardener to look after it.

As I make my painfully slow progress to the back of the house, I can see that there are no lights showing in any of the windows and the house is in darkness. Fen and I agreed that, unlikely as it was, if anyone were awake and looking, it would be strange to have lights blazing in the early hours of the morning. My thoughts return to the noisy revellers in the park; you never know who might be loitering, unseen, watching. When I at last reach the house, I creep along the path that runs along the back until I reach the back door. I test the handle and it moves easily. I open the door and slip inside, pulling the door closed behind me.

Peering through the gloom, I make out the figure of Fen standing by the sink. One of the under cupboard lights is on, giving just enough light for us to see each other.

'He's asleep?' I whisper.

'Yes.' She sounds terrified. I walk slowly across the kitchen towards her, avoiding the large table and chairs, and stand in front of the island.

'You've brought everything?' she asks.

'Yes.' I unzip my pocket and take out the plastic bag with the syringes in. My fingers are clumsy and sweaty inside the gloves and won't seem to work properly. I fumble with the bag but can't untie the knot so resort to ripping it open with my teeth. I place the syringes on the island countertop and shove the plastic bag back into my pocket.

'There are two?' Fen sounds surprised.

'Yes. One should be enough, but I wanted to make sure.'

Fen picks up one syringe and traces her fingers over it. She's not wearing gloves as we planned but

I don't say anything because I don't want to make her even more nervous. Now that I think of it, do we even need gloves?

'Okay.' She puts down the syringe. 'Let's do it.' She walks towards the kitchen doorway and I pick up the syringes in one hand and follow her. We go out into the hall, where she stops and flicks the light switch. The chandelier in the centre of the stairwell lights up and the hall is suddenly ablaze with light.

'What are you doing?' I gasp, blinking and trying to adjust my eyes to the sudden brightness.

'I'm sorry,' Fen says.

'Sorry?' I repeat.

'I didn't want to tell him.'

'Hello Nat,' Darius says from behind me, and I feel the weight of his hands gripping my shoulders. 'How nice of you to drop by.'

I freeze, making no move to get away.

'Take the insulin off her,' Darius snaps at Fen.

Fen comes towards me, and I open my hand wide so she can take the syringes.

'Good girl,' Darius says. 'I like it that you know when you're beaten. Make it easy on yourself because there's no way you'll be leaving here alive.'

'I'm sorry,' Fen says again as she takes the syringes from me.

'Stop saying sorry, you pathetic cow,' Darius snarls at her. 'Go and open the garage door.'

Darius shoves me forwards and steers me towards the kitchen. I stumble and nearly fall and he grabs hold of my arm and hauls me upright, wrenching my arm painfully. I watch as Fen goes into the utility room and I hear the door being unlocked. Darius pushes me along and I stumble as we go through the utility room and through the open doorway into the garage. The garage is much colder than the house and I feel the chill through the material of my hoodie. I shiver, but not just from the cold.

There's room enough for two cars, but only Darius's car is parked in here. There's a clicking noise from Fen, and I look over to see she's holding the car key in her hand. The boot lid unlocks with a clunk and slowly rises open.

Darius pushes me and I lurch forward and hit the back of the car. The rim of the boot digs into my stomach and I fall backwards, landing painfully on the hard concrete floor.

'Get up.'

Winded, I pull myself to my feet, grabbing hold of the car for support. Once upright, I turn and stand with my back against the car. Darius is standing with his arms folded, watching me.

'Thought you were so clever, didn't you?' He grins. 'But Fen always tells me everything, so it was never going to work.'

'I'm so sorry, Nat, I didn't want…'

Darius shouts at her, cutting off her words. 'Shut up or you'll be getting in there with her.'

Fen starts to cry and my insides turn to water as I realise what's going to happen to me.

'You stupid bitch,' Darius spits the words out. 'I knew Fen was hiding something and your pathetic attempt to drug me was so obvious it was laughable. Brett will sleep well tonight because I made sure he drank the coffee that you intended for me. Just as I made sure he drank most of the brandy. You couldn't even tell I was pretending to be drunk.'

I stay mute, aware that there's nothing to be gained by speaking.

'I'm fucked off with you, Nat, to be honest, because I had plans for you and now you've ruined them and that's going to cost me money. I can't trust you now, so you leave me no choice.' He shakes his head and frowns.

'I'll behave,' I say. 'I'll do whatever you say from now on.'

He laughs.

'Don't embarrass yourself. You know you're lying. It's too late. Okay, enough talk. Give me your phone.' He holds his hand out to me and I unzip my pocket and take out my phone. I hold it out to him and he nods at Fen, who steps forward and takes it from me.

'You can get in the boot, now,' Darius says, quietly. 'Unless you want me to force you in there.'

I put both hands on the car and boost myself up and into the boot, my legs dangling down.

'Don't make me say it again,' he growls.

I swing my legs up and in. The boot is so huge that I fit inside with room to spare.

'If you kill me, Brett will go to the police,' I say, my voice quivering with fear.

Darius laughs and then strides over to the car and leans over me. I shrink to one side of the boot, trying to get as far away from him as possible.

'He can do what he likes,' he says, spitting into my face as he enunciates every word. 'Because there'll be no proof. He doesn't even know you're here because Fen told me all the details of your stupid little plan. By the time they find you—*if* they ever find you—there'll be no way to tell how you died because they'll have to use dental records to identify you. There will be no connection to me. Isn't that the very reason you were going to kill me with insulin, Nat? Because it degrades and, given enough time, leaves no trace?'

I don't answer and wrap my arms around my legs to try to stop them from shaking. He shoves me sideways, forcing me to lie down, pressing his arm across my face so that I can barely breathe.

'Fen!' he shouts. He's holding his other arm out to her and I can see as she steps forward. She looks terrified. For the merest beat, I think, and hope, that she's going to stab him with the needle, but she doesn't. She hands it to him. I twist my body around and try to kick out at him, but he grips me even more tightly. I attempt to kick my legs but am suddenly trapped underneath a heavy weight. He's half-climbed into the boot and has stretched one leg over my legs, pinning me down. It feels as if my leg is going to snap.

'Don't worry.' He pushes his face close to mine. 'It's very quick. You won't feel a thing. A prick of a needle and then you'll slip into a coma and die.' He brings the syringe up to his mouth and, putting the needle cap between his teeth, pulls it off.

'Goodbye, bitch,' he says, spitting the cap in my face.

He lifts his arm and I see his enormous fist coming towards me. I feel an excruciating pain in my side as he stabs the needle into me and then almost immediate relief as the weight of his legs is gone. I open my mouth to scream but no sound comes out and I stare up at him in terror.

His grinning face is the last thing I see before my world turns black.

CHAPTER TWENTY-THREE

There's the sound of the door slamming and then silence.

I let out the breath that I feel as if I've been holding forever. They've gone; back into the house. The tension releases painfully from my shoulders and I wriggle my fingers and clench them several times to get the blood flowing. My head feels woozy and I gasp in mouthfuls of air in an attempt to restore my breathing to normal.

I'm not dead.

Yet.

I lie still and as much as the confines of the boot will allow, I stretch each limb to stop myself from cramping. I need to allow myself time to recover and my heartbeat to return to normal before I attempt to get out of here.

Has he really gone? Or is he standing in the

garage waiting for me to get out?

I push the thought away; I'm sure he didn't suspect. If he had, he would have killed me another way. Once Darius had closed the boot on me and could no longer see me, I was too afraid to breathe whilst he was still in the garage for fear that he might hear me. Ridiculous and hysterical, because he couldn't possibly have heard me from inside here but such was my fear, I couldn't bring myself to take the chance. Luckily for me, he closed the lid on me and assumed that I would lapse immediately into a coma and die. Had he stayed around to watch, I'm not sure how convincing I would have been at pretending to be unconscious.

I now have one chance to get the better of Darius and one chance only. Make one mistake and I'm a dead woman.

The syringe of insulin that Darius pushed into my side wasn't insulin as he thought, but vitamin B12. He had no way of knowing that he was injecting me with a harmless vitamin that would do me no harm at all and could, possibly, do me some good. He believed that the syringes I gave Fen were filled with insulin. Although the majority of diabetics inject themselves with insulin pens and not syringes, as a medical rep, I had access to a lot of drugs that the general public don't.

When Fen and I planned to remove Darius from our lives, although I could see that she was totally committed to doing so, I also know how shrewd and cunning Darius is. At times last night

I could sense him studying Fen and I at dinner. He appeared drunk but was he really? The alcohol affected him so rapidly that I couldn't help but be suspicious.

The plan was working so well that it was almost too good to be true.

Which is why I had a backup plan.

I didn't tell Fen my backup plan because if she didn't know, Darius wouldn't be able to make her tell him. It might not work; it's possible that I'll die here, in this house, and no one will ever find my body, but that's a risk I have to take.

For now, I'm alive.

And all I have to do is figure out how to get out of here before Darius comes back and drives me to God knows where and disposes of my body. If he opens this boot and finds me, I don't have a chance.

I feel about in the darkness and slowly wriggle my body around until my feet are touching the back of the rear seats. I put my arms up and run my fingers up and around the back of the seats but the surface is smooth and unbroken by any handles or buttons that would release them. With my back touching the opposite side of the boot, I position my feet on the back of the seats and push as hard as I can, using every bit of strength that I have.

They don't move so much as an inch, there's no give in them at all. After several attempts I decide to stop and save my strength because they're clearly rock solid. I shuffle around again until I'm facing the back of the car and run my fingers around the rim where the boot meets the lid. After several minutes of feeling around me I stop and blink. I can see something in front of my eyes even though it's pitch black in here. Whatever it is, appears to be glowing. I concentrate and a T-shaped piece of plastic a few inches long comes into focus. It's attached to the boot. I wiggle my finger underneath the longest part, grab hold of it and pull. It comes away in my hand. I've snapped it, whatever it is.

But I haven't.

There's a thin cable extending from one end of the plastic and I grip it tightly, and pull. There's a clunking noise and the lid of the boot pops open. I lie still for a moment before pulling myself up and peering through the narrow gap.

The garage light is still on but there's no sign of Fen or Darius and I can see through the gap that the door to the utility room is closed. I stay still and listen.

Silence.

I quickly push up the lid and clamber out, pulling the boot lid down and closing it behind me. The clunk sounds deafening as it closes. I run to the front of the car and crouch down behind it, out of sight. I wait for the sound of running feet and shouting but there's only silence.

Taking a chance, I stand up and stretch. I don't know how long I have before he comes back but I'm guessing that Darius won't want my body in his garage for very long.

He could be back at any minute.

I take my baseball cap off, easing it carefully over my ponytail. It's a tight fit – which is the reason I wore it – because I didn't want there to be any possibility of it falling off. Once the cap is off, I put my hand inside it and carefully remove the thick tape covering the crown. Tape removed, I'm relieved to see that the two syringes it was holding in place are undamaged.

These syringes do have insulin in; one syringe-full should be enough to kill Darius but I'm taking no chances. Belt and braces. I intend to stab him with one syringe and once he's weakened, inject him with the second.

Any misgivings I may have had about murdering Darius have vanished; he was fully prepared to kill me without a moment's hesitation and I feel no guilt for what I intend to do. Although truthfully, if I'm completely honest with myself, I had no misgivings even before he forced me into the car boot. Darius's visit to my bedroom convinced me beyond doubt that he would carry out his threat to make me disappear into a life of sexual slavery and misery.

There is only one way out of this mess, and that is to kill him.

Checking the caps are firmly on the needle tips, I slip one syringe into my pocket and hold the other in my hand. It's not lost on me that it's all very well having the weapon, I now need to actually inject it into Darius without him overpowering me and using it to kill me.

The only advantage I have is surprise. He thinks that I'm dead or in a coma and won't be expecting me to attack him. I look around the garage and debate the best thing to do. When he comes back in it's going to be via the door from the utility room. He'll need a spade or some sort of tool to dig a grave, or at the very least, something to cover me with, and I can't see him opening the garage door to the driveway until he's ready to leave.

I quickly run past the car and towards the utility room door, praying that Darius doesn't choose to come back right at this moment. I stand in the corner of the garage, directly behind where the door will open. When he comes in, he won't know I'm here and I can jump out and push the syringe into him before he knows what's going on.

I rehearse it in my head; I need to push the syringe into his stomach if I possibly can because it's the softest place. If I push it into his leg or arm, there's the possibility of the needle snapping against his muscle or, if I manage to inject him through the muscle, the insulin will take longer to incapacitate him.

It would have been so much easier if he'd been asleep.

I hold the syringe in my hand and hold my arm up, trying to judge how high I'll have to hold my arm as he comes through the door. Do I stab him immediately he comes in or run after him as he walks to the car? What if he's wearing a coat?

The needle won't go through a coat; he could be wearing a coat if he intends leaving immediately because it's cold outside. The probability of success now seems remote in the extreme and as I consider my imminent death, the sound of the door lock clicking enters my consciousness. The handle on the utility room door begins to turn.

I slowly lower my arm and with trembling fingers, pull the protective cap from the tip of the needle. The cap tumbles from my fingers towards the floor as if happening in slow motion. The door is opening and I watch in horror as the cap hits the floor at the exact moment Darius's foot emerges from the doorway.

He's going to see it.

I'm dead.

He doesn't notice it; he steps into the garage and walks without hesitation towards the car. Fen isn't with him and I wonder where she is.

I can't worry about that now.

He's dressed in a t-shirt and jeans, thank God, no coat.

Will the needle penetrate the t-shirt?

When I planned this, I never thought of any of this and it suddenly seems stupid and foolhardy to even try. What if the needle snags in the t-shirt? What if Darius grabs my hand and I never get the chance to stab him with it?

I could run; I could wait until he's driven off and run for my life.

It could work.

Except I'd have to keep running forever and Brett would have to run, too.

And if Darius looks in the boot before he drives away then I won't get the chance, anyway.

It's already too late; he has the car key in his hand and I hear the beep as he presses the button and the clunk of the boot lid as it starts to slowly rise.

It's now or never.

I tear across the garage, my trainers making little noise on the floor. It's only as I reach Darius that he senses my presence and spins around to face me. Our eyes lock for a millisecond before I thrust my arm towards his stomach and push as hard as I can, pressing the plunger on the syringe as I do so. He looks down in surprise, before grabbing hold of my arm and twisting it painfully away. The syringe is still sticking out of his stomach and he takes hold of it with his other hand and pulls it free, hurling it to the floor.

Did the insulin go in?

I attempt to twist my arm out of his vice-like grip but it's impossible to squirm out of his grasp. Grabbing hold of my ponytail, he wrenches my head back and spits into my face.

'You fucking bitch.'

He releases my hair and grabs me roughly around the neck with both hands and begins to squeeze. I try to prise his hands away but my fingers make zero impact on his vice-like grip. I punch him in the chest but my hands bounce off as if I'm hitting a brick wall. I can't breathe and my chest feels as if it will burst out of my chest and there's a buzzing noise in my ears. My neck feels as if it's about to snap because he's squeezing so hard. My legs buckle beneath me and as I slip into unconsciousness, my last thought is that I didn't give him enough insulin.

Except that I'm not unconscious.

I hit the floor, my hip hitting the concrete painfully, gasping for air. Darius falls with me and as I land, he's lying on top of me, flattening me.

But his hands are no longer around my neck.

With difficulty, I try to push him off me and he mumbles something that I don't catch. With all the strength I can muster, I push his shoulders, twisting out from under him at the same time, scrambling as far away from him as possible.

Once I've got my breath back, I stand up on shaking legs. He's lying motionless, only his mouth moving, as if he's trying to speak, but there's no sound coming from him. I unzip my pocket and feel around for the syringe, praying that it hasn't broken in the fall. I pull it out of my pocket and hold it up in front of my face. Black floating circles swim before my eyes but I see that, miraculously, the syringe is intact. I have an excruciating headache but I ignore it. He could wake up, he could recover; I have to do this *now*.

I take the cap from the tip of the needle and kneel down next to Darius.

This is how it ends.

CHAPTER TWENTY-FOUR

'Have you heard from Fen at all?' Brett asks, as we're eating breakfast.

'No. Why?' I carry on pretending to read the news on my phone, feigning disinterest.

'No reason. Just feels odd that Darius has gone so quiet. I haven't even seen his car about. Are you sure Fen went away on her own and he didn't go with her?'

'Don't know.' I shrug. 'That's what she told me. Said she was going to visit her family and Darius can't stand them, so he was staying at home. Maybe he changed his mind and went with her.'

'Hmm.' Brett picks up his slice of toast and inspects it. 'I'm surprised he let her go on her own. Thought he wouldn't let her out of his sight. I reckon he must have gone with her.'

'Maybe. But who cares? Because wherever he is,

he's leaving us alone, and that's a good thing. With a bit of luck, he'll stay away forever.'

'I wish.'

I don't answer and continue to study my phone as if it's absolutely fascinating. It's Saturday morning and the silence from Darius, as they say, is deafening. It's bothering Brett; he's heard nothing from him for a week and the lack of messages and prompts about the financial information Darius wants is giving him hope, yet unsettling him.

Fen really *has* gone to visit her family. She's staying with her sister and nephew, who she's barely seen for the last ten years. Fen normally keeps away from them because Darius doesn't let her go alone and she refuses to inflict his bullying ways on them. He's alienated her and made it all but impossible for her to see them. I told Brett that the visit was planned and that Darius knew about it, but of course; he didn't. I lied that we'd discussed it over dinner last Saturday night and the reason he can't remember the conversation is because he was so drunk. He couldn't argue; he commented it must have been strong brandy that Darius was dishing out, because he can barely remember a thing about that night. As the week has gone on, he's said several times he thinks his drinks were spiked. I agreed with him because he's right, even though the sleeping tablets weren't meant for him.

I don't tell Brett that Fen will be returning home

today because he'll find out soon enough.

Then it will begin.

The lies.

What happened a week ago seems almost unreal now; at times it feels as if last Saturday were a horrific nightmare. By not speaking about it, I can pretend that it never happened.

Because Brett knows nothing of what I did, and I'll never tell him.

What would be the point in him knowing? It's better that he doesn't know. I'm protecting him by not telling him the truth, but mostly, I'm protecting myself. I didn't tell him because I don't want him to know what I did.

Or what I'm capable of.

He would look at me differently; I'd no longer be the girl he married. At first, he'd be massively relieved that Darius could no longer threaten or control us, but as our lives return to normal, he'd look at me and wonder why I didn't tell him what I planned to do. How could I do something like that? The questions would start; the demand for all the details.

I'd look like a cold-blooded murderer.

Which, I suppose, I am.

He'd see me that way, too, eventually. And maybe become a little afraid of me and imagine what I might do to him if we ever fell out of love. No. I won't tell him for the same reasons I didn't tell Wendy about Griff. If she knew Griff was in the house when I started the fire, she'd consider it murder, not luck, that he was dead.

Some things should never be shared.

I did what I did for the best of reasons, but it was still murder. Fen knows what I did, but once this is over, we won't ever have to see each other again. We've agreed that we won't be friends and we won't make any attempt to contact each other. We both played a part in Darius's death, and even though I was the one who killed him, Fen was complicit.

'I'm going to wash the car.' Brett gets up from the table and goes out to the garage and I hear him clattering around, getting his cleaning stuff ready. The car isn't in the slightest bit dirty, but I know he needs something to concentrate on; to take his mind off Darius. I can see the nervousness building in him. At first he was relieved that Darius was leaving him alone, but now he's worried. He's afraid he's playing a game and will demand even more from him when he eventually contacts him. I desperately wanted to tell him he didn't need to worry anymore, to put his mind at rest, but of course, I couldn't.

It won't be much longer now.

I think back to last Saturday night, how Fen came into the garage and found me standing over Darius's body minutes after I'd injected the second syringe of insulin into him.

I was so relieved to see her.

She had a swollen eye and marks around her neck where he'd throttled her, but she was alive. If

I hadn't killed him, there is no doubt in my mind that Fen would be dead by now.

And I would, too.

But as it is, we're both free of him.

She ran over and threw her arms around me and we stood and hugged in silence in the cold garage while we gathered the resolve to do what had to be done.

We knew that to make his death look accidental, we had to move him. By that time, he was dead. Maybe he was already dead when I injected the second syringe into him; I'll never know because I didn't check. We struggled to move him because he was so heavy; I think he must have weighed more than the two of us put together. Standing either side of him, we took hold of him underneath the armpits and dragged him into the house, through the kitchen and hallway and into the lounge.

It took hours.

We had to keep stopping to rest and to recoup our strength. We thought that once we'd got him into the lounge, the worst of it was over, but we were wrong; getting him onto the sofa was nigh on impossible. We managed it, but were both sweating and exhausted by the time we'd finished. It had to be done because we wanted it to appear as if Darius had accidentally overdosed. The police would wonder why he'd gone into the garage to take drugs when he had an entire house to sit in. It needed to be convincing, and we had to get him into the lounge to make the story work.

When Fen returns home from visiting her sister today, she'll find Darius dead in the lounge and she'll call the police—after she's turned the temperature down on the central heating thermostat. It won't be pleasant for her to find him because he'll have been lying there for a week. Before Fen left for her sisters, she turned the thermostat up to a tropical temperature so that the house would be extremely warm. If Google is to be believed, his body will have decayed much more rapidly than if we'd left it in the cold of the garage. If all goes well, the decomposition will be so far advanced that they won't be able to determine the exact cause of death. The insulin in his body should have dissipated to the extent that it's untraceable. If they find any trace of drugs at the post-mortem, it'll be the heroin that Fen and I injected into his arm once we'd got him into the lounge. We scattered heroin and drug taking paraphernalia on the coffee table next to the sofa and a shoelace will still be in place, tied around his arm. Fortunately for us, Darius kept a large stash of drugs in a holdall in his wardrobe, which Fen has always known about. Darius wasn't an addict, and as far as Fen knows, he wasn't a dealer, either. She said he rarely took drugs himself, as he preferred alcohol, but would occasionally snort cocaine. The holdall contained cocaine, heroin, tranquilizers and Rohypnol.

I shudder to think what he had them for.

Fen is going to lie and tell the police that

Darius was a regular drug user; cocaine mostly, but sometimes heroin. I'm hoping the police and coroner conclude he died from an accidental overdose of heroin. If everything goes according to plan, they'll be satisfied that it was an accident.

If we're unlucky and the police make house to house enquiries and any of the neighbours' security cameras caught me when I returned home, they won't know it was me. I kept my face pointing downwards, away from the cameras and all they'll see is a figure dressed in black out for an early run.

And anyway, it couldn't have been me, I was at home in bed.

It was just after seven o'clock on Sunday morning when I slipped into bed next to Brett. He was still sound asleep because of the sleeping tablets he'd unwittingly taken that were meant for Darius. Had he woken, I had an excuse ready; I'd been downstairs and made myself a cup of tea because I had a headache and I needed to take some paracetamol. As it was, I didn't need to use my excuse, because he never woke until past ten o'clock. He was groggy and hungover and spent the day complaining that he couldn't understand why he felt so ill because he didn't think he'd drunk *that* much.

I gave him a wry look and asked him if he'd forgotten how ill he'd been in the night. He stared at me in disbelief as I told him he'd been up at three, throwing up all over the bathroom and that I'd spent an hour cleaning up after him. He was apologetic and said he couldn't remember any of it, but after a while, said he thought he vaguely remembered feeling sick and vomiting everywhere now that I mentioned it. I reinforced the lie by telling him I'd forgive him for the mess as long as he promised never to get so drunk again.

The perfect alibi.

The only evidence from that night were the finger marks left by Darius around my neck. Covered up with polo necks and high collars, the marks aren't visible and the weather is still cold, so wearing high necks doesn't look suspicious. The marks are so faint now as to be almost gone, but I'm taking no chances; I'll be covering my neck for a few more days.

The police should have no reason to suspect foul play. Fen will tell them she's been staying with her sister and thought that Darius was away on business abroad. She'll say that he rarely contacts her when he's away, so she wasn't concerned when she didn't hear from him. If questioned further, she'll then reluctantly admit that they led mostly separate lives and that their marriage wasn't good. She'll also hint that he had other women. She'll tell them, honestly, that he went away for days at a time and she never knew where he was going or who he was with.

She sounded positive, telling me what she's going to say to them. I wanted to believe she'd be strong, but I couldn't help remembering how

Darius knew she was hiding something from him. She must have guessed what I was thinking because she said it wouldn't be like lying to Darius, because she's not terrified of the police. I just hope she doesn't lose her nerve because if she does, I'll be forced to defend myself.

Clearing the breakfast dishes away and loading up the dishwasher, I wish that today was over. I run upstairs and change into my running gear, making sure my top covers my neck. A run is a necessity today because I'm jittery and unsettled and if I don't do something, I'll drive myself insane.

I come downstairs, put on my trainers and open the front door. Brett is laboriously polishing the already pristine car in slow, circular movements with a look of concentration on his face. With a false cheery wave, I jog past him and head towards the park. From across the street, the driveway of Fen and Darius's house shouts its emptiness at me as it has done every day since Fen left. A mental picture of it crowded with police vehicles and dozens of uniformed police bustling around flashes into my head. I swallow down the panic that threatens to engulf me and race past their house and through the entrance and into the park.

I've run around this park so many times this week that there should be a groove of my route in the path. Each time I've been here, I've been trying to dispel the memory of last Saturday night from churning around in my head on a loop.

I wonder if it'll ever stop.

I've not allowed myself to think, or have any hope, about the future, because everything is riding on how well Fen lies to the police. She's well aware that I can easily incriminate her if I choose to; there are no witnesses to attest to who gave Darius the fatal injection. If forced, I'll inform the police that I witnessed Darius abusing Fen and she'd confided in me how much she hated him. This will give Fen a motive, whereas as far as the police are concerned, I don't have one. Brett will testify that I was in bed asleep all night, next to him, and he'll recall that he was ill, and I had to clear up after him.

The outlook would be very bleak for Fen, and I'm hoping that it never comes to that. Because I don't think I can do the noble thing and accept the blame for murdering Darius; if it comes to it, I'm going to throw Fen under the bus.

Because, as I've always known, I'm not a good person.

All I can hope is that Fen is as strong as she says she is.

When, or if, this is all over, I'm going to suggest that we move house. I don't think for one minute that Brett will want to stay here. I don't care where we go, as long as it's away from this street. Darius has tainted this house and everything to do with it.

I continue my sprint around the lake, running ever faster with each lap as if I can leave all of it behind, but, of course, I can't. When I can't run any further and have a stitch in my side, I head towards home. As I come out of the park and into the top of our street, I see a car driving towards me.

It's Fen.

I slow down and watch as she turns onto their driveway. I jog down the street and as I pass their gateway, Fen is climbing out of the car. I put my hand up in a wave and she raises her hand towards me, her expression blank.

We lock eyes for a second and then I turn my face away. I cross the street and turn into our driveway, my heart suddenly pounding.

It's begun.

CHAPTER TWENTY-FIVE

There are two for sale boards on the street; ours, and Fen's.

Fen is no longer living there; she moved out of the house the same week that Darius was found dead. She messaged me to say that she was going to stay with her sister and nephew until she had sold the house and then she'd look for a new home for herself.

I never replied.

I haven't heard from her since. We'd exchanged a brief flurry of messages in the days after she arrived home, but once the police left her in peace, I thought it best to cease all contact. I haven't actually *seen* her since the day I saw her getting out of her car, and I have no intention of ever seeing her again.

I needn't have worried about the police being

suspicious; they never doubted Fen's version of events at all and Darius's death was recorded as an accidental death. They informed Fen that the inquest, which won't be held for some time, is simply a formality as the evidence speaks for itself.

We never went to the funeral. I looked at the online local newspaper births and deaths to see when it was, but I had no intention of attending. I only looked because I needed to know where to send the flowers and I didn't want to ask Fen. We sent a medium-sized wreath; exactly what we'd have sent if one of our other neighbours in the street had died.

Although obviously we weren't sad; we were over the moon.

It's not nice to celebrate a person dying, is it? I don't mean rejoice in their life and achievements, but celebrate the fact that they're dead and gone forever and are never coming back.

Brett booked a table at a really expensive restaurant and we had the most perfect meal, accompanied by an expensive bottle of champagne from the wine list. We toasted the fact that Darius was dead, and that we'd never have to see him again. We couldn't keep the grins from our faces and we didn't even feel bad about it; he deserved to die.

We'd got our lives back.

In that moment, as we chinked champagne glasses, I was so tempted to confess what I'd done, but I stopped myself. I knew that the relief I'd feel would be short-lived and that Brett would start with the questions and they'd never end. In time, I can forget what I've done, or if not forget, think about it less and less so I can live with it. I buttoned my lip and agreed with Brett that it was truly fortunate that Darius accidentally overdosed.

Once Darius's death was old news and the funeral was over; we waited a few more weeks and then put the house up for sale. We discovered it had actually increased in value in the short time that we've been living here, so that was a bonus. After receiving several offers over the asking price, we accepted the highest and expect to move within the next couple of months.

We've already found our new home, which is not too far from here, and we're moving up the property ladder much sooner than we thought possible. Our offer has been accepted for a house that would perfectly fit Brett's old life plan, if he still had one. With the increase in value on this house and Brett's annual bonus, we can easily afford the new mortgage, even without me having yet found a job. And with moving and all the work that entails, we've agreed that we'll get settled in the new house before I begin my job search.

Or maybe I won't bother looking at all; maybe we'll start that family straight away.

Our new house has an enormous garden with a high brick wall that goes all the way around it as well as rather grand electric gates at the entrance. We laughingly call it 'our castle' because it really is our dream home and I can't see us ever wanting to move again. The nearest houses to it are too far to walk to, so there's little chance of us bumping into anyone. They're not close enough to be properly called neighbours, so we're on our own, away from other people.

Which is fortunate; because I've killed twice and I don't want there to be any reason to do it again, because one more would make me a serial killer. So we won't be making friends with any new neighbours, ever again.

It's much safer that way.

For everyone.

THE END

Thank you so much for reading this book, I really do appreciate it. I do hope that you've enjoyed it and if you have, I'd be thrilled if you took the time to leave a review or star rating on Amazon/and or Goodreads.

Made in the USA
Columbia, SC
18 April 2023